MIZ LIL&
THE CHRONICLES
OF GRACE

OTHER BOOKS BY WALTER WANGERIN, JR.

As For Me and My House
The Book of Sorrows
The Book of the Dun Cow
A Miniature Cathedral
The Orphean Passages
Potter
Ragman and Other Cries of Faith
Thistle

MIZ LIL&
THE CHRONICLES OF GRACE

WALTER WANGERIN, JR.

1817

Harper & Row, Publishers, San Francisco

Cambridge, Hagerstown, New York, Philadelphia, Washington
London, Mexico City, São Paulo, Singapore, Sydney

Library of Congress Cataloging-in-Publication Data

Wangerin, Walter.
  Miz Lil & the chronicles of grace.

  I. Title.   II. Title: Miz Lil and the chronicles of
grace.
PS3573.A477M59   1988   813'.54   88-45159
ISBN 0-06-069267-7

89 90 91 92 RRD 10 9 8 7 6 5 4 3 2

Contents

79386

And those who are good—they delight to hear of the past evils of such as are now freed from them, not because they are evils, but because they have been and are not. With what fruit then, O Lord my God, to Whom my conscience daily confesseth, trusting more in the hope of Thy mercy than in their own innocency, with what fruit, I pray, do I by this book confess to the people, also in Thy presence, what now I am [against what I have been]?

—Augustine, *The Confessions* 10.3.4

EASTER-WINGS

Lord, who createdst man in wealth and store,
Though foolishly he lost the same,
Decaying more and more,
Till he became
Most poore:
With thee
O let me rise
As larks, harmoniously,
And sing this day thy victories:
Then shall the fall further the flight in me.

My tender age in sorrow did beginne:
And still with sicknesses and shame
Thou didst so punish sinne,
That I became
Most thinne.
With thee
Let me combine
And feel this day thy victorie:
For, if I imp my wing on thine,
Affliction shall advance the flight in me.

—GEORGE HERBERT

Author's Note

The stories told in this book are true. They happened. And most of the characters you will encounter here are also accurate portrayals. But I've made an aesthetic and ethical decision sometimes to conflate events, sometimes to create a single fictional character from a composite of many people, and sometimes to invent the detail and the character which the deeper spirit of the story required. In this manner I've tightened the pace of a human life considerably, and I have absolutely rejected using details or identities which would disclose another human life besides my own.

Preface

A wandering cleric was my father.

Wherever he went I went there too, as rootless as he was in this world. But there came a time when I turned and traveled in ways he never chose, and then we were divided for a while.

I was born in Portland, Oregon, the first child of a youngish Lutheran pastor and a woman of eager intensities: dramatic, enthusiastic was my mother's hunger for the world. And she was handsome in those days. One mute snapshot shows an even, intelligent brow, a sparkling eye, and a widow's peak.

Within a month of my birth, my pastor-father baptized me. He prepared for the rite by warning the deacons not to worry if the baby should cry from the shock of the water. "A lusty lung," he said, half joking, "means my son is destined to preach." But I remained serene throughout the ceremony. I uttered not a peep.

After the service—so my father told it—the deacons met him "with faces as long as hoe-handles."

"We're sorry, Reverend," they said.

"Why?" said my father. "What's the matter?"

"Well, your son will never make a pastor," they said.

The baptism took place in Vanport City, Oregon, where I lived the first year of my life. I remember nothing of Vanport City—except that we returned there thirteen years later to view it from a hill, and found that it had been lost entirely to a flood. Nothing built remained, nothing but the flat grid of empty streets and grass.

We moved. I spent my second year in Shelton, Washington. My mother once said that we could see Mt. Olympus from the kitchen window, but I don't remember Mt. Olympus. On the other hand, it is during this period that personal memory begins for me—sudden, sharp, and seemingly pointless—and I do recall a sighting of the Pacific Ocean.

This memory starts as we are driving a narrow highway through tall, continuous forests of pine. I have made a bridge of my body, my toes on the back seat of the car, my arms and chin on the ridge of the front seat, my face between my parents' faces. They are gazing forward through the windshield. My father drives. My mother is talking— though memory preserves neither the timbre of her voice nor the words; rather, I see the tip of her nose dipping down as her mouth keeps forming soundless sentences. Forever and ever that tiny trick of her nose consoles me when I watch it, proof of my mother's presence.

Then my father says, "There!" I hear the cordwood tone of that command. "Look to the left," he says. "You'll see the ocean."

Almost casually I glance left. The forest is thinning as we speed through it, and a distant water flashes between the trees. Suddenly the pine is altogether snatched away, and I am startled by the sight. There, indeed, lies the monstrous sea, a nearly impossible reach of water, massive, still, impersonal, and infinite.

"I rowed a boat out once," my father says, still looking forward, "and swam in the Pacific."

My mother shudders.

I imagine my father in that boundless water, a dishrag beside a bobbing rowboat, and I shudder too.

This is where my earliest memory ends.

We moved again—to Chicago, Illinois, where my father served the youth organization of the whole church body. His wandering increased in distance and frequency, but he traveled alone. The rest of us spent portions of the hot, hot summers with my mother's family in St. Louis, Missouri.

Dramatic was my mother's hunger for the world, enthusiastic; but the world would not hold still for her; therefore her enthusiasms were forced to turn in upon themselves. And as the forms of my father's religion did not change, however much we wandered, the forms themselves became a sort of moveable stability and structure for our lives; and my mother—deep-hearted, brave, a warrior for the sake of the homeland, had there been a homeland—guarded the doors of religious form as though it were the fortress that kept her family safe. We were the Jews, whose Sabbath and whose circumcision were bound to no particular place, though their hearts might long intensely for a city.

We moved again. Before I enrolled in the third grade, my father had entered the pulpit of a parish in Grand Forks, North Dakota.

Now we lived in a windy old house above the banks of the Red River. Our back yard ran down a hill of weed to the wood that bordered the water. In spring this river burst its banks and rose to cover half our hill, then descended, leaving a blackened vegetable growth that disappointed my mother's sense of order and beauty. She waited till the ground grew dry again. She waited while weed entangled the whole of the hill. And then one day she took an ancient, clattering push-mower and attacked the ugliness. Back and forth, back and forth with a sort of fury she mowed and mulched the humid weed, leveling the growth, by will alone prevailing. I watched her and said in my soul, *This is a very strong woman.*

By midsummer the weed returned, and rabbits lived in it.

We moved again.

My father accepted the office of president for a small preparatory school, many of whose students went on to the seminary and then into ministries like those my father had served.

We lived in Edmonton, Alberta, Canada. The winter shocked us with its cold, then held us in its everlasting cold. The North Saskatchewan River, whose valley the front of our house oversaw, froze solid. And for several years my mother suffered certain chill indignities which I could not understand. In that place, then, the fortress of our faith grew stronger, stonier, more embattled; and I would watch my mother's eyes, sometimes, and marvel at their icy perseverance: the hard blue guardianship which would, by God, maintain the protective structures of this family's safety. And I would want to cry for her.

We moved again. But with this move we separated.

My parents and family returned to Chicago, while I, the firstborn of my father, attended a boarding school in Milwaukee, Wisconsin, a high school like the one he had administered, a prep school for the Lutheran ministry.

I too, it seemed, would prove a wandering Aramaean like my father.

And I did go wandering—but not in the obvious, geographic way my father took. In fact, I had already departed from my family several years before I left them for Milwaukee. Nobody knew my leave-taking, least of all myself: the spirit of this nomad was invisible. But quietly—as my family struck camp again and again—secretly, unknowingly, I had decamped the faith.

I lived still within the forms of my father's religion. My mother's fortress still surrounded me. And so far as I knew, there were no reasons why I should not also march the walls of the stronghold of Christendom. It was without a conscious deception that I planned to become a pastor.

But form was form alone; the law alone was real; and I had stolen out-of-doors to wander another sort of waste.

Half of the stories that follow in this book recount that hidden journey of the spirit of a child. Into Egypt, one might say.

And then—despite my silence at the baptism, despite my distance from the heart of the faith of my parents (but nothing is as simple as that statement sounds, and I was valiantly ignorant even of myself)—I was ordained into the ministry. I did, as a young man, start to preach.

But if my father had moved continually, I would stick in one place only. Early in adulthood I began, as the pastor of a small, black congregation called Grace, to preach; and I stayed there: in the center of Evansville, Indiana, on a northward loop of the Ohio River.

Yet if my father had never deviated from the still center of one consoling creed, his firstborn had. Ever in Evansville, the invisible spirit of this nomad had very far to go. Out of a deep unknowing. Out of his Egypt, learning to walk.

And a frozen river must break before it flows again. But a summer of constant hearts can accomplish this terrible wreckage.

Half of the stories in this book observe that other journey—of the spirit of a young man bound to a particular people, a spirit bound to Grace.

It will help the reader, perhaps, to know that these two series of stories are presented alternatively, first the adult, then the child, the adult again, the child again, and back and forth as once my mother went back and forth to level the tangled weed until her hill was beautiful.

1

Derelict

"Petals, Reverend?"

"What?"

The man startled me from my thoughts, though that wasn't his intention. He was frowning into the rearview mirror, watching the line of cars that crawled behind us.

"I'm sorry, what?" I said.

"Petals or dirt?" he said, returning attention to the road ahead. "What's the Lutheran tradition?"

I closed my mouth and looked forward too. I fingered the black book in my lap. Everything was feeling like a test these days, and every test had its trap; and though Mr. Lawrence George was the most civil of men, conducting his business merely, the question embarrassed me. I didn't understand it.

Two cars passed on the left. A pickup labored by, muttering smoke.

We were traveling north on Garvin, a one-way street which, with the parallel south-running street called Governor, gave access through the inner city of Evansville. Mr. George drove at a grave rate, slowly, slowly, never more than fifteen miles per hour. Generally motorists raced these streets, trying to hit the stoplights green, then shooting the stretches between as though the city streets were country highways. Even now the vehicles passed us in clots of two and three at a time. But Mr. George maintained our dignified crawl as the difference between mindless haste and old decorum.

He had solemn reasons for driving slowly. He was a man

with a ramrod commitment to ceremony and deep convictions of propriety. The car he handled was a Cadillac, long
and low and black. The car behind us was a hearse. And
each of the seven cars that followed the hearse displayed a
purple flag on its fender. We were a funeral procession: he
was the director.

"Reverend?" he repeated, giving his eyebrows a delicate
twitch, gazing forward.

Mr. Lawrence George was the funeral director. I was the
pastor. And the woman in the hearse behind, she had belonged to Grace Lutheran Church—an old, old soul only
lately come into my care. We were at the end of her mortal
age and the beginning of my mortal ministry: this would be
the first interment for the both of us.

"Petals? Or a handful of dirt? Lumps of earth?" said Mr.
George. "You're in charge, sir."

"Ah," I said.

We were approaching Walnut Avenue. Mr. George did not
speed up. Neither did he slow down, though the stoplight
was red against us. He closed the distance with unshakable
serenity, driving, driving, while I trod the floorboard under
my right foot.

"I don't," I said, clearing my throat, "I'm afraid I don't
know what we're talking about."

Mr. George began to sound his Cadillac horn and entered
the intersection against the light. "D'you plan to say 'Ashes
to ashes'?" he said over the organ of his horn. The traffic
on Walnut, both on the left and on the right, was forced to
stop and to stay stopped for the slow succession of cars that
followed us. I avoided the drivers' faces. "Do Lutherans say
'Dust to dust'?" he asked, releasing the horn, still gazing
faithfully forward.

"Yes, I think so," I said. "Yes, we do."

"So then," he said, "d'you want me to drop petals on the
casket then? Or clay? Different preachers have different notions, but I am yours, sir, to see it's done in dignity."

"Ah, yes. Dignity."

Mr. Lawrence George sat erect beside me, the knot of his tie projecting bravely from his throat, the rest of the tie disposed within his vest, a man as dignified as Immortality.

"Yes," I said. But I had never considered the question of petals-or-dirt before. I didn't know that such a question existed. There were suddenly so many questions to consider. What *do* the Lutherans do? What do the blacks do when they mourn? What do *I* do when the cultures collide? People remember these things forever, especially funerals, especially the funerals that failed and gave offense somehow. Oh, Lord! I did not want to be in charge. Maybe *The Pastor's Companion* contained an answer to petals-or-dirt. But neither did I want to look like I wasn't in charge by checking the black book in my lap. So then: wing it.

"Wouldn't dirt," I said, "make a sound? A truer sound, I mean? Symbolical—a hollow rattling sound?"

I'm certain that Mr. George would have responded, then, with an opinion—but he didn't have the chance. Suddenly he stiffened at the wheel.

High and whining behind us, screaming in low gear its furious impatience with slow decorum, a stripped-down Buick came passing the entire funeral procession in a single, angry acceleration. It cut in front of the Cadillac, shifted, vomited at the tailpipes, and roared ahead.

Mr. George compressed his lips and allowed his eyes a momentary diffusion; but he did not vary our funereal pace.

He counted cars in the rearview mirror. He stroked the steering wheel with his left hand, and then expelled his breath.

"There was a day, Reverend," he said. He grew more formal with the quiet declaration. "There was a day when folk respected the dead, when they rose up in pity with the mournful." Mr. George had a neat, close crop of iron-white hair: light-skinned, pressed, and proud. He glanced at me a fleeting second, then seemed to make a decision in my behalf.

"I remember that day," he said, gazing forward, nodding.

"Reverend, I remember when construction workers on Seventh Avenue stopped their riveting as we drove down the street. They laid their tools aside, they stood in lines on the lofty girders, they covered their hearts with their hats, and they dignified our grieving, yes. I saluted them. They stood like soldiers in the sky." He lifted his chin, remembering. "It didn't matter what day it was when the casket passed. All the days were Sunday for a funeral. And I'll tell you another thing too. It didn't matter what color we were, driving to the graveside, no. Didn't matter what color the folk on the sidewalk sported neither. They paused respectful. Death had one color in those days, sir. Bereavement had one color only." He breathed through his nose a moment. He had elevated his face until the line of his sight went down his cheeks. "Black," he said.

He shook his head. "Everything's changed today."

Mr. Lawrence George fell silent.

I looked out of the side window. I felt my nerves grow tighter in the silence. The gravity of this man's remembering lay burdens on me that I could scarcely bear. Nothing was light. Everything required a heavy rectitude—and I was the pastor in charge. Ah, Lord, the office was so much older than I was. Petals or dirt? And how many people would be affected by the choice I made? I hardly knew these people. Petals or dirt? Well, well—then let it be dirt.

We had driven far north of the inner city by now. Garvin and Governor joined to form a single two-way street called Stringtown. Here on my right was a busy high school, the students pouring forth for their lunch hour, the curious students peering in our windows, mugging. I turned my face forward again. There, ahead of us, was Diamond Avenue, four lanes of a nearly constant traffic, a median dividing the lanes.

But Mr. Lawrence George made no concession to modern thoroughfares. He caught a yellow light at Diamond, sounded his Cadillac horn, and kept on driving, slowly,

slowly. He made a left turn, west on Diamond. He drew his sad train slowly through a red light, while on every hand the cars of the city hit their brakes and stopped.

Three young girls suddenly broke from a knot of students, threaded the stalled traffic, and dashed across two lanes of Diamond to the median. For a few moments they raced with us. Then all at once they lined up in a little-maid row and waved and smiled and clapped as we drove by. We were their parade, a noontime entertainment.

"Everything's changed," sighed Mr. Lawrence George.

In the cemetery some twenty men and women gathered quietly beneath a yellow canopy.

The coffin rested on a shining device above its hole. As though it were a confidence between the two of us, Mr. George tapped the end where the woman's head was enclosed. Propriety put me at her head, not her foot. I took my place at that end, then, and waited, feeling sweat on the cover of my black book, *The Pastor's Companion*. A breeze flapped the fringe of the canopy.

Six members of the immediate family arranged themselves on a row of folding chairs to my right. They gave particular consideration to one who was the daughter of the deceased, an elderly woman herself, sagging in sorrow, sagging in all of the lines of her face, leaning on the arms of a nephew and a niece in order to lower herself and to sit.

Two weeks ago we had laughed together, this woman and I. We had laughed at the fact that she had but a single personal tooth in her jaw, more precious to her than a pearl— and when the dentist suggested he ought to pull it, she bit him.

She kept her head down now. It seemed to me that we should look at one another sometime before this mournful day was done. Pastor and parishioner in sympathy together. Perhaps we were avoiding the direct glance. I myself—I think I feared it. I had hardly known her mother, dead at ninety-two. What would I have in my eyes to give the daughter, should she look at me?

But then, none of the bereaved was looking at me now. Arms were folded on their chests, lips pushed out in meditation.

Mr. Lawrence George stepped to the foot of the casket, removed a single marigold from the bouquet, began to crush it in his left hand, and with his right hand saluted me: erect and military, his duty discharged. He meant, *Begin.*

I did. I lowered my head and read from the black book, pinching pages against the breeze.

"We brought nothing into this world," I read, "and it is certain we can carry nothing out. The Lord gave, and the Lord hath taken away—"

My voice lacked resonance out of doors. The wind scooped and billowed the canopy.

When I reached the words, "O Death, where is thy sting? O Grave, where is thy victory," the daughter of the woman who had died began to cry. At first she just said, "Hooooo. Hooooo," and compulsively I read a little faster. But then a great gout of grief broke from her throat.

"Mama!" the woman wailed, throwing her hands to the top of her head. "Oh, Mama!"

I glanced nervously among the faces. No one seemed terribly distressed. The niece and the nephew were patting her shoulders and fanning her with cardboard fans from the funeral home. Others were rocking side to side as if hearing a music.

I ducked and read on: "Forasmuch as it hath pleased Almighty God, in his wise providence, to take out of this world—"

Suddenly the woman drew a shuddering breath and shrieked, *"Mama, Mama!"*

I shot a pleading look to Mr. George; but he merely

pursed his lips, closed his eyes, and nodded that I should continue.

Hasty and nervous and gripping the book like a banister, I continued: "—out of this world the soul of our departed sister, we therefore commit her body to the ground; earth to earth, ashes to ashes, dust to—"

"*Mama, you gone! Oh, Mama, you*—" The poor old woman simply erupted. She rose from her chair. Her mouth gapped black. Her dentures dropped, dead-grinning, to her chin. She made a gurgling sound and passed out backward in her nephew's lap.

In that same instant I saw that Mr. Lawrence George was with unshakable serenity scattering marigold petals on the coffin lid. Not dirt! The skin of my face burst into flame. I felt in the midst of everything a sudden, speechless fury. I thought I had told the man *dirt!*

Driving back to the funeral home, Mr. George cast off his solemn mood and relaxed. He grew talkative, sunny even. I myself—I could not speak. I glared through the side window and fingered my moustache.

When we crossed Walnut southward and entered the inner city again, the mortician grew positively expansive.

"I used to deliver newspapers here when I was a boy," he said, another sort of remembering, I suppose. "See that house down Cherry?" he said. "The two-story house with cornices? That woman never missed a payment, summer nor winter, three years straight," he announced. "But she shot her husband dead with a single bullet while he stood at the top of the stairs. What d'you think, Reverend?" He glanced at me. "Maybe it was passion gave her the aim?"

In the parking lot of the funeral home, I broke out of the Cadillac and strode to my own vehicle, a small Toyota pickup truck, and threw myself inside.

"Reverend! Wait a minute," Mr. Lawrence George sang out, with interminable slowness rising from his longer, blacker car.

I turned the ignition. "I've got to go," I said.

"You'll do all right here," he declared as though I hadn't spoken, as though I wanted his approval. "Stay tender, sir," he called, touching his hand to his forehead in that formal military salute. "Stay as tender for folk as I saw you today, and you will do all right."

I shifted into first. "I've got to get back to the church," I said.

"Oh—wait!" He suddenly bent at the waist and reached into the Cadillac. "Wait!" His voice was muffled in the dark compartment, but I heard him say, "Your Bible!" and I didn't even answer that.

Wrong, sir. I had taken no Bible with me.

I accelerated, muttering Toyota smoke.

I drove west to Governor, then turned left and joined the traffic streaming south. One-way street. I kept in the extreme left-hand lane, my tires eating the pavement just inches from the curb, telephone poles switching past my ear. Go! Go! Go!

Grace Church was on Gum Street, one block east of Governor. But before my turn I had two stoplights to negotiate, one at Lincoln just ahead, the other two blocks farther down at Bellemeade. I sped up. I intended to hit both lights green, because if you got stopped by one you'd certainly have to stop for the other. The sequence was very tight.

Immediately on my right was a silver Chevy traveling at the same speed as I was. Evidently it planned to catch a green at Lincoln too. A race. I sped a little faster. So did the Chevy, vexing me.

But together we did it. We hit the stoplight yellow, in fact, and cleared Lincoln in a double bound. Two blocks to Bellemeade. Bellemeade was waiting green. Go!

But then I lowered my sight and saw an obstacle ahead.

I squinted. At the end of the first block was an old man sitting on the curb, his legs and his upper body bent directly in my tires' path. Idiot!

I had two choices: step on the brakes and stop, or step on the gas and beat the Chevy to that fool, veer to the right, and miss him. The old man gave no indication of moving or even of noticing us. I beeped.

In compressed time I saw him with a frightful clarity. He was thin, unkempt, hunched forward so that his head hung down between his knees. What then? Drunk? His clothes were wretched. On the pavement between his shoes lay something vividly red. He was staring at it. I felt enraged by this utter indifference to danger, which forced me in the middle of my busy day to make decisions on *his* behalf. Oh, the indigent are so arrogant! Why didn't the man reach down and snatch the damn bandanna between his feet and get out of my way? I beeped. I beeped. He didn't budge. I chose speed.

All in a hurtling instant, furious for what he made me do, I down-shifted, mashed the accelerator, caused my Toyota to whine ahead of the Chevy on my right, swerved away from the old man's knees, and whipped his pantlegs with my wind. I gave him a wicked, accusing stare as I shot by— and I took, in that stare, a picture that only slowly developed in my mind.

That red bandanna was crawling the ground as though alive. Threads of red were hanging from the old man's chin. The man had just begun to raise his face, and I saw that his mouth was also smeared with red. No, no—this was no bandanna at all. It was blood. The old man was vomiting blood in the gutter. Jesus!

The light at Bellemeade met me green. I took it numbly, then slowed to make the turn at Gum. How was I to know? How was I to know? The silver Chevy blared its horn as it roared on south down Governor and was gone. I didn't respond.

I pulled up in front of Grace Church and sat in the Toyota with my forehead on the steering wheel. Trembling. I couldn't stop trembling. I sat for a long time trying not to tremble, but failing.

For God's sake, how am I supposed to know these things?

Suddenly someone rapped on my window, and I jumped.

Mr. Lawrence George.

The funeral director stood outside my pickup truck, erect and formal in a three-piece suit, serene and smiling. He showed me that he was carrying a black book in his hand. He opened my door and extended the book to me.

"Reverend," he said, bending a bit for a bow, "you forgot your Bible."

"No sir! No sir!" I snapped. "It is not a Bible. No sir!" I grabbed it from him. My hand shook. "It's called *The Pastor's Companion*."

I stepped out of the pickup and walked toward the church, almost mute with fury because I could not stop myself from trembling.

2

The Spittin' Image

My mother was kneeling on the floor in the dining room. I stood directly in front of her, face to her face. She was gazing at me, eating me in big bites with her eyes.

"Wally," she whispered, nearly a sigh.

Suddenly she leaned forward and seized me to herself. She hugged me with my arms straight down and printed her tears on my cheek. She had been crying.

"Oh, Wally, Wally," she murmured into my neck. She kissed me. Then she sank backward on her heels and shed a glittering smile upon me. There was a clear drop clinging to the end of her nose. I had the fleeting thought that she would burst out laughing—on account of the pressure of her smile. She didn't. Instead, she said, "You are the spittin' image of your grandpa."

This is the first time I ever heard that expression.

But my poor mother seemed overcome by the thing she had said. Her face dissolved to tears again, even while she kept gazing at me. She whispered moistly, "Yessir, yessir, child: the spittin' image of Grandpa Storck."

So she said—and then I wondered what the "spit" was.

I was six years old, a trooper in the first grade, the oldest kid in my family, and quick at the mysteries of words. I had the immediate sense that "image" meant I looked like Grandpa, which flattered me because I loved the old man. The big man. The man with wild white hair like Moses on the mountain and a face as severe as the tablets of stone. It was good to think I looked like Grandpa, an elevation of sorts.

But I didn't know what the "spit" was. That disconcerted me.

Oh, Grandpa was a wonderful man to "image." Superintendent of the cemetery in St. Louis, he was: master of the green lawns walled around with brick to six feet high; watchman, warder of the scattered stones, the gracious trees, the winding roads, the memorial shrines in which the memories were enclosed; king of the sleeping kingdom was he, to whom I was the green and golden prince—I the huntsman and herdsman as well, and grandly happy. Grandpa shot red squirrels when I visited him in the summers: single shots, most accurate pops in the silence of the cemetery. He skinned them and I watched him hang the pelts in the basement of his house, which was also on the cemetery grounds. And this is how strong the man was: during Prohibition (so my mother told me) he was called to the little illegal saloons that certain Germans maintained in the neighborhood around the cemetery. When Louie had a drunk he couldn't handle, big Bill Storck strode into the oily darkness (ah!) and lifted the drunkard bodily, like a basket of cabbages, one hand at the poor man's collar, one hand at his belt. Then he strode outside again and across the street to the cemetery wall, where, with little effort, he slung the drunkard up and over six feet of brick. And my mother said that Grandpa said: "Let a *Säufer* wake on a grave, and see if he changes his ways."

My mother grew pink with pleasure remembering such stories. And she said I was the "image" of this man, whom she obviously loved, whom I loved and honored with all my heart. It was good to be a little image of Grandpa Storck.

But the *spitting* image of the man?

It made me nervous, thinking what the "spit" was.

Well, Grandpa chewed tobacco.

Was there some custom of which I was ignorant that

grandsons must take the places of their grandfathers, to chew tobacco on behalf of the whole family—and to spit? Grandpa spat. Would his spitting image have to spit?

The prospect dried my mouth out. I didn't fancy chewing on the old man's quid.

Besides, I could never match my grandpa for spitting. I didn't think anyone could. Grandpa Storck was an athlete at spitting. 'Twas an admirable, breathtaking thing that he could do.

Moreover, he loved me, did my Grandpa Storck, the solemn Lord of the green lawns and the gravestones. He loved me. And this was his particular way of showing love for me, by spitting. No, I simply could not imagine duplicating the *meaning* of the marvelous act.

Marvelous? It was a spectacle of skill, performed for me alone; and the more skillful he, the more love for me, since the finer was the gift that I was given.

Grandpa seldom smiled. He had an eruption of moustache beneath his nose, like white smoke from the chimney pots of his nostrils. His face was mostly expressive of one mood only: solemnity, rectitude, Lutheran doom. His arms were long and strong, his hands huge, his stride unhalting, his whole body an uncompromising dogma. Moses! Grandpa Storck, his hair like cloud at the top of his head, was an immediate Sinai, grim and untender—but I was not intimidated.

For *this* Mount Sinai could spit.

This old man, he loved me in the spitting.

For we would be sitting in his study, as dark and oaken as Lutheran truth. For he would be massive behind his desk, while I kept silent in the corner, according to his admonition. For he would flick me a sudden, significant glance, and I would recognize a break in the weather, and my heart would leap, but I would strive to keep my face as solemn as his. For he would clear his great throat and creak backward in his swivel chair, backward, *backward* until his face was

aimed toward shadows at the ceiling, toward some spot so
high above his brass spittoon, itself three miles away from
him, that no one would bet a nickel he'd hit it. For I would
fight the giggles in me, trying to be worthy of the grand
occasion. For Grandpa—angled backward in his chair,
twitching his mighty moustache—was Olympian.

And Grandpa spit.

Ha! but there was a splendor in that rising, shining, dark
brown spew—and a glory so important that everything
moved slow-motion to my sight. Listen: the goober never
touched his moustache! It rose from his lip like a darker
comet with a long, delirious tail. It ascended the air of his
study in reckless daring: he spat *up*, not down. He spat *distance*, not safety. This was no timid dribble. This was the
audacity of outrageous skill. High in space that comet would
curve into a perfect apogee, then suddenly tip and sail
downward with a gathering, giddy speed—till, *Poooom!* it hit
the target center-brass, *Poooom!* a ring of triumph. Done.

And Grandpa would flick me another glance from his spit-
position in the chair, and that undid me truly. I laughed out
loud in spite of myself. I shouted. He had done it, and he
loved me, and I acted like a kid for what I'd seen, laughing
pure delight and gratitude.

But Grandpa brought his body forward then. He brought
down the frown upon his eyes and restored sobriety between
us. He would growl, *"Halt's Maul, Junge!"* and I did. I shut
up. But I sat with my ears stuck out from grinning.

So we would walk the kingdom together, he and I. And
he would stride, but I would run to stay abreast of him; and
the summer was hot, but the day was always lovely, and I
was happy as the grass was green, oh, I was lordly in the
rivers of the windfall light. My grandpa, the Keeper of this
cemetery, the rule of all the world, he loved me.

And twice that I remember, my grandfather smiled at me.

Once we stood at a distance from some people gathered
beneath a canvas canopy—they in their Sunday best, mur-

muring words around a coffin, we in our boots and overalls, waiting by the shovels till they spoke a last Amen and we could go to work. I felt superior since those strangers had come at our behest and stood at a hole we'd dug, we and the workmen, six feet deep. This was our province. We would be here when they had dispersed. My overalls felt like a uniform, a privilege outranking their suits and their dresses.

While we waited, Grandpa began to talk. His very voice had whiskers in it. He kept his eyes on the murmurers at the grave, but he gave me his leisure; he chose to disclose to me the mysteries of Death.

"*Junge*," he said solemnly. *Boy*, he said in the German tongue, pursing his lips so that the moustache dropped a heavy wisdom.

"Grandpa?" I whispered.

He chewed in silence a moment. I knew better than to interrupt even the breathing pauses of his talk. Between the murmurers and us a mound of earth had been covered by a tarpaulin. Neat squares of sod were stacked beside that.

"*Junge*," he said, "did you know that a dead man, he don't die all at once?"

"No," I whispered.

"*Ja*," he said, chewing. "It's a *seltsam* fact of nature. I have seen the proofs of it. I myself have opened the coffins. Little things live on."

I looked up at his eyes, the eyes that had seen. I looked where he was looking, at all the Sunday people bowing heads around a coffin. I gazed steadfastly, then, at the coffin itself, curiously wrought with hinges and handles. A body was in there. "Am I," I whispered, "a little thing?"

"*Ein kleine Bengel*," he declared.

"Ghosts live on?" I suggested, feeling the twist of excitement in my tummy.

"Parts of the body, *Junge*," he confided. "Even buried, parts of his body live on." He was calm and solemn, imparting such information to me. But I grew breathless, approaching the mysteries.

He flicked me a measuring glance, then gazed away and grunted. "I have seen," he said, "the hair of the corpses, long and tangled in the tombs, still growing in their graves—"

Wow! I began to grin, seeing the same thing.

"I have seen," he intoned, "yellow toenails curled around the feet like claws. It's the hair and the nails that keep on growing. *Ja.*"

Wow! With my eyes I tried to drill into the coffin over which the Sunday people were praying. What would those people say if they knew what I knew now? Intoxicating knowledge! Or what would they do if I opened the lid? The hair and the nails—wow!

"*Junge?*"

"Grandpa?"

"Do you know the big word *cremation?*"

I did. I felt very proud that I did. "Burning dead bodies back to dust," I said, more breathlessly than ever. I felt that my face was shining beside this man, before his exquisite secrets. But he was keeping his face earnest and professional, his great hands behind his back, observing the people at their distance. I could hardly stand this. I put my own hands behind my own back and gripped them hard and tried to frown.

"Well," he said, "when they burn the bodies, they close the furnace doors. And do you know why that is?"

"No?" I peeped.

"Because the dead," he said, "they sit up in the fires and scream—"

"*Wow!*" I shouted right out loud. That picture popped my eyes with an astonishing insight, and I lost control. "*Wow!*" I bellowed, and all the people at the graveside stopped praying and turned to stare at me.

Instantly I glanced at my grandpa—and there it was.

Though he was watching the Sunday people still, in his

eyes there appeared a sudden twinkle, and under his moustache: a smile. It was as suddenly gone; but while it shined, it was a grin of cunning satisfaction. He bowed grandly at the staring people as if to say, *So, have you met my grandson?* and he continued to gaze at them until they turned away again.

"Whisht, whisht, *Junge*," he said to me with a surprising tenderness in his voice, "there is a perfectly scientific reason for this. Fire expands the air in the lungs, you know. Leftover air, you see. It rushes through their throat-boxes, so they scream. And it tightens their muscles, so they sit. Reflex, ain't it?"

That was the first time that grandpa smiled for me and bound me to himself. Twice he smiled. I remember them both as treasures.

But the second was not a cunning smile. The second was purely kind.

One afternoon that very summer when the sun grew round, my grandfather honored me by showing me a place which no one knew but him, which no one used but him—and even he reserved this place for extremest need. Near a shed that smelled of oil and hay, in a corner between two fences—one of them wooden and one of them brick—my Grandfather Storck introduced me to the wall against which, when he simply could not wait to get back to the house, he peed.

And thus it was that sometimes that summer we stood side by side, my grandpa and myself, solemnly facing the same wall in a wordless fellowship, bowing our heads as devoutly as though we prayed, but peeing. This was a holy moment, and I knew it. For we were man and boy together, little and large, absolutely intimates, members of a proud society, and in love.

My grandpa's prayers lasted longer than mine. My grandpa's capacities were in every way a wondrous flood, mine but a trickle. No matter. This hard and stolid man, this Moses

of the wild white hair, this Lutheran of inflexibilities and
spit—he loved me enough for both of us. I know. I know.

For once when we were done, when I had heaved a sweet
and shuddering sigh, he turned and looked directly in my
eyes. And he smiled.

And then one afternoon in Chicago I returned from
school to find my mother in my bedroom, busy, busy, distracted. "We have to visit Grandpa," she said.

She said "have to" as though it were distasteful to her. In
fact, she was packing my clothes in a suitcase and all her
gestures seemed sharp and angry to me. And because it was
my clothes in her hands, the anger seemed aimed at me.

I said, "Why?"

She gave me an angry look. "What's the matter?" she said.
"Don't you want to?"

That's not what I meant. I always wanted to visit Grandpa.
I said, "Well, but I'm in school now."

"Call it a vacation," she said, punching a wad of socks into
the suitcase.

Vacation? My mother never relaxed the rules. Only something extraordinary could persuade her to change patterns
or plans already fixed.

But school isn't what I meant either. I think I meant: *Why
are you angry?* But that's too hard a question to ask entirely,
so I just said, "Why?" I think I meant: *What's wrong, Mama?*
And I surely meant: *Why don't you look at me?*

I said again, "Why?" And since I had no other words but
these, I said, "Why do we have to visit Grandpa?"

She frowned. She glowered. She said, "Nosey children lose
their noses."

"Mama?" I said. "But why?"

"Because he's dying, Wally, all right?" she snapped. "Is
that good enough for you?"

"Dying?" I whispered.

"Dying. Yes, dying. Cancer," she said, as though she were answering a stupid question. She slammed the dresser drawers.

But I wasn't asking a question. I was just confused by the word "dying." I thought I knew the word. Grandpa had already taught me about dying; but he spoke wonders and mysteries. Now my mother spat the word like a bile, and suddenly I didn't know "dying" at all. What was this "dying" that my mother should be so angry about it? Something was terribly wrong—and the fact that she wouldn't look at me frightened me, because I feared that somehow I had done the wrong.

"Mama?" I said. This was not good judgment. I probably shouldn't be talking now because I'd make things worse. But I needed to know something and I couldn't help myself. "Mama?" I said. "What's cancer?"

"Tumors," she said. *Whap!* "Sickness," she said. *Whap! Whap!* She was trying to close the suitcase. It wouldn't shut.

"No," I said. "No, but what do you *do* for cancer?"

My mother raised her eyes a hot second and burned me with a look. Once more she tried to shut the suitcase but failed. "Oh, Wally!" she cried. She slammed the lid so hard that my shirts bounced out. "Oh, Wally, just leave me alone!" she cried. She left the room.

So then I understood that I was a guilty person, though I didn't know why. And I knew that dying must be very horrible, though I didn't know now what it was. And I understood above all things that I had better be quiet, had better keep still and do as little as possible, because anything I did might be wrong. Nobody had prepared me: *What is right? What do you do for this sort of dying?* I didn't know.

For the rest of that day I tried to make myself as small as my baby brother, as hidden as the mouse. I didn't like it that I was the oldest. My body felt gross and clumsy in this atmosphere. I wished, in fact, that I could disappear.

At sunrise the following day we were gone. We drove the

long road from Chicago to St. Louis in a killing silence. Silence, as I understood it—silence was either parental disappointment or parental impotence before enormous badness. I shrank and shrank in the back seat of the car. But I could not, finally, become nothing. I couldn't make me not be there. I kept my head against the windowglass and closed my eyes and pretended to be asleep.

In St. Louis I watched the city go by. I found that I felt very sorry for all of the people that I saw.

And then the cemetery, when we entered the iron gates, was not the same. It was quiet. It was under governance of a grim adulthood, no longer green nor golden, annexed: the childless land. Cars like husks were scattered around my grandfather's house.

We went in the back door. The kitchen had high ceilings and cupboards with windows so that you could see the dishes inside of them. Aunts and uncles greeted my mother with murmuring, and all were severe, and all of them angry, and nobody noticed me, for which I was grateful. Where was Grandpa? If anyone noticed me, what would I do? How should I behave? The dying I didn't understand was in this house, thick like a smoke, like the smoke of a burned food— shameful. But what it was, and what you do for it, no one had taught me. Where was Grandpa?

With a strict gesture and a meaningful step, my mother led me from the kitchen through a little hallway, through the dining room and into my grandfather's living room. There was a cot in that hallway, covered with white sheets; and a man was under the sheets. At first I thought that it was Grandpa. But there was time for only a glimpse, and then I thought that it wasn't Grandpa because it didn't look like him.

My mother made sure that I sat on the sofa, and then she left me among the cousins, all of us silent. We didn't look at each other. I didn't swing my legs as I sat. I didn't know what they were thinking, but I was thinking this: *If you don't know what to do for dying, do nothing. Say nothing. You'd only make it worse.* Where is Grandpa?

What is cancer?

I did not cry. I folded my two hands in my lap and sat in a private trembling, voiding my face of everything.

And then it was that my Grandfather Storck remembered me.

My mother returned to the living room, but I didn't see her. She touched my shoulder, and I jumped.

"Grandpa wants to see you," she said.

I got up and followed her in mute obedience, not even unfolding my hands. We went back through the dining room, into the little hallway. My mother moved behind me and put her hands on my shoulders, positioning me before the cot which was covered with white sheets, and then she left me, and I was standing fixed to the floor, staring at the man beneath the sheets.

My heart beat in a sort of panic, and I thought, *Is this what dying is, that people are not the same anymore? They become— someone else?*

The man before me was bones, old bones and nearly no strength on those bones, but a yellowed sacklike skin.

I could neither move nor speak. I looked. No one had told me what to do.

The man had a moustache as yellow as straw, nose holes huge and black and empty, a yellow face with the cheeks sucked in, the temples sunken, the poor eyes covered with a paper skin, thin, translucent, oh! His long arms were longer than Grandpa's and skinnier. His hands were wider than Grandpa's; they lay on his chest like empty shovels. The breathing whistled in his nostrils. He stank. His hair stood up like a wild, yellow fire—

And then the man moved.

He rolled his head in my direction. He allowed his eyes to open, and he looked at me, and he said nothing at all, but he did this: he smiled.

I drew a sudden breath, and released it in a word: "Grandpa," I whispered. "Grandpa, it's you."

For everything else may change in mortality, everything except this one thing: the smile that love engenders. And then nothing else is important anymore. Grandpa smiled and suddenly this was my Grandpa Storck. And he smiled at me, so I was there as well. In a flood I felt a freedom, I felt me come to be, and I grinned so that my ears stuck out. We were there in the room together, companions, man and boy, little and large, his Moses hair and mighty moustache, my silly, impossible giggling.

"Grandpa!" I said.

"*Junge*," he smiled.

And then, without another word, he taught me what this dying is; and he taught me what you do for it. He invited me to himself. Having loved me when we walked the green and golden ground together, even now he disclosed the final mysteries to me, and he loved me to the end.

The smile faded. Solemnly the old man raised his right hand from the sheets and reached in my direction. I understood the invitation. I knew what to do.

I walked to him and stuck out my lesser hand. He took it and held it in his—and he did what you do for dying. We shook hands. He shook my little fist with a dignified, sober ceremony, first up, then down: Once. Twice.

I learned. I did not tremble, and I did not cry, since I learned not only what you do for dying, but also what it is. It is leave-taking.

I said, "Good-bye, Grandpa."

And under the cloud of his moustache the old man moved his mouth. He smiled.

All this is right and true.

How long was it later? I don't know. It can't have been more than two weeks. My mother and I were sitting at lunch in the kitchen of our house in Chicago. We were eating soup. The telephone rang, and I looked quickly at her eyes. There are times when you know the message by the ring itself.

My mother stood up and went into the dining room, where the telephone was attached to the wall, shoulder-level. I watched her go. But I knew already what she would hear.

She lifted the receiver and put it to her ear. She said some words, and someone said words to her. She bowed her head while she was talking, and she pressed her left arm against her stomach. When she was done speaking, she kept her head bowed, leaning forward until her forehead touched the wall, and she stood that way, utterly silent, her eyes closed, replacing the phone by habit. Grandpa was dead. I knew that someone had just told her that her father had died. I also knew immediately what to do.

I rose from the kitchen table and walked into the dining room.

"Mama?" I said. I stood at her left side. She didn't hear me.

I tugged her skirt. "Mama?" I whispered. She opened her eyes and looked down at me. Then I did what you do for dying. I stuck out my right hand.

Slowly my mother reached down and gave me her own hand. I gripped it in a fine strong grip, and with a dignified, sober ceremony I shook my mother's hand, first up, then down: Once. Twice.

This was clearly the right thing to do. Because with the second handshake, I brought my whole mother down upon my shoulders. She covered me with a pure and holy hug, and she allowed herself to cry on me, softly, softly, and I didn't mind because this was my job now, because I had learned and I knew and was able: my Grandfather Storck had taught me.

In a little while her sobbing subsided. My mother kneeled down and gazed directly into my eyes, looking, searching. She kissed me. She smiled a glittering, smile upon me, a rainy sort of gladness, and I thought she might burst out in laughing. She didn't. Instead she said, "Wally, Wally—you are the spittin' image of your grandpa."

And I began to wonder what the "spit" was.

Or whether I had to chew the quid my grandpa chewed before he died.

Some twenty-seven years thereafter I was sitting in another kitchen in another city altogether, Evansville, in the home of one of my parishioners.

The woman across the table from me was Musetta Bias, a strong-boned, strong-hearted woman as capable of love as any of my forebears, but nowhere near as stern in Lutheran rectitude. Lutheran she was. German she was not. Musetta was black. Her love had no hard edges.

We drank tea together on that particular day, because we had only recently buried her husband; and, though the committal service had been smooth and gracious and (she told me) comforting, there'd been no chance for personal words at the graveside. Arthur had died of a wasting cancer. He had been a big man, a police officer, a man who liked his green beans cooked with bacon fat.

We were spending a holy moment remembering him.

Suddenly Musetta turned her face to the window.

"Arthur Junior," she said, speaking as though their son were just about to enter the room. "Arthur Junior," she said, "is the spittin' image of his daddy."

No! No, she did not say "spittin' " at all.

I nearly lunged at the poor woman.

"What did you say?" I said.

She blinked at me.

"Musetta, what did you just say?"

"I said," she said, "that Arthur Junior is the spee-it 'n image of his daddy—?"

"Did you say 'spit'?" I demanded.

"No," she said. There was Southern blood in the woman, ancient roots to the language in her mouth.

"You didn't say 'spit'? Spit? Like spittle, spit?"

"No," she said, backing away from my intensity. "I said 'spee-it.' "

Spee-it, dear God! That's the way the South elides its syllables, swallowing Rs in the process. *Spee-it* is *spirit*. Musetta was saying *spirit*. Arthur Junior was the spirit and image of his daddy.

That's what the spit was.

. And my mother, whether she knew it or not, had said no less. I did more than look like Grandpa Storck. His spirit, the character and the force of his being, dwelt within me. When I put forth my boyhood hand to touch her, why, it was as well the hand of her father. Her father had come consoling her, not gone at all, not altogether gone, abiding in his grandson, one.

Even so had the child, still young and easy, received like clay the impress of an old man's love. Death was not division in that summer, in the sun that is young once only.

Junge! Did you know that a dead man, he don't die all at once?

And the boy, before he followed time from grace, said, *Yes, old man, I know.*

3

Miz Lil

1.

Douglas Lander drove the mule that pulled the plow that broke the earth to dig the hole on which was built Grace Lutheran Church. They dug that hole twice. The flood of 1937—when folks boated above such streets as Governor and Garvin—filled it in the first time. But Douglas was ever an even-tempered man and would do the same thing six times over uncomplainingly if five times first it failed.

"You can't command a mule," he chuckled even to the end of his days, "until you got its attention. An' you know how you get a mule's attention?" It was a tired joke; but Douglas was so sweet in its delivery, so pacific a man himself, so neat and small a ginger stick, that people grinned on the streets when he told it. He was a pouch of repeatable phrases. Besides, it was understood that he meant more than mules: the younger generation, the government, some recalcitrance in human nature, cocky young preachers—whatever the topic of his present conversation. He could trim a joke to any circumstance. "Hit it with a two-by-four."

He wore oversized glasses with silver stems. He never learned to drive a car. He walked wherever he went, and he paused to talk with whomever he met. And quietly, confidently, as though it were the deeper creed of her soul, Miz Lillian loved him. Miz Lil. She was his wife primevally. Her loving needed no public demonstration. She had been there before he drove the mule that pulled the plow that broke the earth—twice.

Both Miz Lillian and Douglas—and she was as short as he was, though neater, thriftier, quiet, maternal—were fixtures of the inner city neighborhood, as standard as pepper shakers on a table. They *made* the mean streets neighborly. They gave the crumbling streets a history. Douglas could point to a rubble three blocks west of Grace, where the city had demolished some substandard house, and remember: "I lived there. Right over there. And I recall when Line Street *was* a line, black to the west of it, white to the east, and you better not cross 'less you got business takes you across. Now we black on both sides." He grinned. He lifted his sweet eyebrows. "One o' them things," he sang high tenor. "One o' them things."

Miz Lil spoke less of the past than did Douglas. Not because she did not remember, rather because she spoke less than Douglas in all things. She hadn't a compulsion to talk. She watched and kept her own counsel, and her words were weightier, therefore.

But Miz Lil remembered slippers in the Depression, how that Douglas once came home with a box of pairs of slippers, payment for an odd job when jobs were scarce. She remembered the distribution of slippers among their relatives and friends—and chickens, when they got them, and canned goods. And the slippers may not have been terribly warm in winter, but they were a sort of bank deposit, a sort of security, because some relative might earn an extra coat and a friend might find some precious article like long underwear—and then Douglas, who hated the cold as perhaps his only enemy, could dress the warmer in consequence of the slippers.

These were the flesh of the inner city, Douglas and Miz Lil, the living ligatures. For their sakes, do not call it a ghetto. Do not presume it a mindless, spiritless, dangerous squalor—a wilderness of brick and broken glass, brutality, hopelessness, the dead-end center, no! They made it community because they remained in confidence and honor.

The *Lamed Vavnik:* the Righteous Ones. They gave it civility, familiarity, and purpose—they caused it to be a good ground on which to raise fat children—because they remembered the names.

"Her grandma's name was Alice Jackson," said Miz Lil. "Come up from Kentucky with her family when the coal mines couldn't support them. Turn of the century. She went to school with me, Alice did," said Miz Lil, remembering, the veil of time upon her eyes. "Bright. She was bright in those days. With stories and plans, all eager for the future. But then she got caught raising children, and then her children had children, and she raised them too. And she suffered to feed her grandbabies. She put on weight. I remember how Alice Jackson labored to breathe, surrounded by grandbabies. But she suffered to make them good too. Took them to church, yes. Prayed to Jesus for their souls. She did the best she could. A body can only do so much. When you talk about skinny Marie," said Miz Lil, "you think on her grandma, fat Alice Jackson; then you can't help but talk with pity, and you'll be inclined to give Marie a drink of water for her grandma's sake. No, you won't be judging Marie then. She's got good blood in her and the print of love in her poor face. The fat just closed on Alice Jackson's throat, I think. I think it got to be more misery to breathe than not to. That's how she died, I think."

In the context of such remembering, how could the inner city be faceless, rootless, cruel? Concrete and desperation only?

Under the sunlight of such a mercy, how could anyone, smug in the suburbs, fear it as dark and dangerous?

This was no ghetto. Douglas and Miz Lil—invisible perhaps to the outside eye for that they blended in; who were black and short and old, who held no office but had lived there since the beginning of the world, when folks swept not only their porches in the morning, but their sidewalks and their gutters too—Mr. and Miz Lander, they were its citizens.

He wore long underwear, autumn and winter and spring, laughing at himself because his little body could not endure the cold, African indeed.

She trudged to the projects with pies and helped move Mrs. Collier's furniture out on the lawn so they could bomb her place for roaches. Mrs. Collier needed comforting for the incomprehensible disruption of her life. Mrs. Collier also needed a bath.

They wore, did Douglas and Miz Lil, the mantle in the neighborhood. They scarcely knew this; therefore they wore it in a perfect modesty; but perhaps any community with blood ties and past history and present complexities, problems that want a personal solving, contains one or two wise spirits, sages to whom the rest of the people will come when they are themselves at wit's end and helpless. Upon these the mantle has fallen. These Wise Ones are chosen unconsciously, by the mute agreement of the truest members of the neighborhood. They are invested with a silent respect. The community is stabilized—the community is both grounded and elevated also and comforted—just knowing that the Wise Ones are there. Whether one ever takes advantage of their presence or not, one knows he has a place of appeal: *Somebody knows my name.*

But to eyes outside that small society, the mantle is invisible.

Who would ever talk about it?

To hearts within the small society, it is a consolation taken for granted. No one would ever talk about it.

Nevertheless, it is nothing other than prophecy. It is the presence—the *bath qôl,* the living voice—of God.

Douglas Lander died while watching "The Lawrence Welk Show" and eating a piece of pie. Miz Lil was dozing on the sofa at the time. She didn't realize that he was gone until the house had filled with a perfect quietness and she saw him slumped all wearily on the floor. Perhaps he'd been coming to tell her something.

His glasses, those wide temples and the silver stems of them, had always seemed too big for his filbert face, too formal for a man so sweetly malleable to all the sudden circumstances of this existence. But when he lay thoughtfully in the casket, the glasses seemed absurdly superfluous. And the suit that they had dressed his body in, it was too big at the neck, excessive at his thin wrists and little hands.

At his wake the people noticed the lack of long underwear and chuckled over homely jokes. "He be warm now, Miz Lil," they said. "He got God for sunlight now, and it ain' nothin' but summer where he gone to."

Miz Lillian barely acknowledged the joke.

She stood at the bier of her husband, rubbing and rubbing her abdomen, a little woman gazing at a little man now lost in thought.

She would have to do the talking now. One pepper shaker stood alone.

In the months that followed, Miz Lil did not interrupt the habits of an old, old life. In the evening she sat behind screens on the porch of her house, facing Bellemeade Avenue, watching the traffic. Watching nothing. Sometimes relatives sat with her. Sometimes not. She gave the impression of rocking, whether the chair could rock or not, because she maintained a slow, perpetual rhythm in her body, a secret drumbeat. In fact, she was rubbing her stomach with one hand or with both.

On Sundays she went to church. She sat in the second row from the back on the left-hand side, the same pew that the Lander family had always occupied since the mule first plowed the ground and the little building had been built. She didn't sing the hymns. Neither did she, who had never been demonstrative of deeper feelings, demonstrate her feelings now: her face was internal, her eyes were like tiles of porcelain.

In this wise did she take her place among the people after worship, and file through the tiny narthex, and shake the pastor's hand.

The pastor leaned down to her and spoke as if no one else were there. He said, with earnest significance, "How are you, Miz Lillian?"

She responded as if no one at all were there, neither the pastor, whom her tile-eyes did not see, nor even herself. "Fair," she said. That was all she said. She proceeded through the double doors outside, holding her stomach with the hand the pastor had just released.

And so the year unraveled.

Douglas and Miz Lillian, complements of one another in character, behavior, and in wisdom, once had worn the mantle together. It was uncertain—though no one consciously asked the question—whether Miz Lil would lay it aside now altogether, or pull it over her head and hide in sorrow, or else wear it for the people's sake alone. If she did not wear it, it would be quietly cast upon another, whom slow time, the passage of a thousand days, would reveal. Or if none other received the mantle, that would be a sure and terrible sign of the breakup of this small society. But if, in time, she lifted her face and smiled again and spoke to someone a consoling word, then God would not have left the inner city without its prophet, would not have left the people without *bath qôl*, the daughter of the voice of God.

The end of this story is this:

On a particular evening the pastor came to visit Miz Lil in her living room. While they sat together, he on the sofa, she in a rocking chair, rocking and rubbing her stomach at once, dark grew darker in the room and the faces of both of them dimmed to the other's sight.

The pastor prayed a prayer. That is what Miz Lil had said he could do for her. But he ran out of prayer before he ran out of yearning on the little woman's behalf; so he sat in silence.

And then she broke the silence. Miz Lil began to talk. The pastor listened without interruption and slowly began to realize, even before she was done, the holy benevolence of her words. In the darkness he allowed himself to cry.

In fact, Miz Lil was speaking of grief. Carefully, touching the subject with infinite reverence, she said that her grief was a stone in the womb. Not *like* a stone, no. It was there—a lump as mortal as an infant between the wings of her old hips, but heavier: a painful, physical presence. "And you pray it would go away," she said. "It doesn't go. You plead to Jesus you can't bear the suffering. You bear it anyway."

She rocked and rocked in the darkness. There was the sound of a whispering fabric: she was rubbing her stomach.

"Finally you understand," said Miz Lil, "that this is the way it's going to be forever till you die. The stone is never going to pass. You're going to mourn forever. But you say, *This isn't wrong.* Finally you say, *This is right and good.*"

The sorrow that started as the enemy, it ends a friend. This is what Miz Lil explained as the night developed. Sorrow had become a familiar thing for her now, and the perpetual pain in her stomach a needful thing. It was there when she woke at midnight, there in the morning. She took it to church with her, and she brought it home. This particular baby would never be born nor ever leave, but would companion her forever. This was the loneliness that kept a widow from being altogether lonely—because it was, inside of her, a memorial of her husband. It was pain and wanted rubbing. It was sorrow and caused her to sigh. But it was also the love of Douglas—and stroking it was the same as stroking the husband whom you love.

"Douglas is not far from me," said Miz Lil, "nor me from Douglas—" In midsentence, she fell silent. There was only the sound of the whispering fabric. And the pastor in the darkness realized his tears.

More than that, he understood them. For he wept for the old woman whom he loved, whose sorrow affected him, but whose resolution of the sorrow kept his tears from being merely hopeless. For he wept as well for the neighborhood at large, because this marvelous, holy talk of Miz Lillian's was a sign: she had taken the mantle up again; she had found a way to wear the mantle not altogether alone. The voice of God had not departed from the grim streets; the inner city had its Wise One still.

For he wept, most particularly, for himself, because the woman had chosen to speak such intimate wisdom to him, to reveal her inmost spirit to him. He was, therefore, no more a stranger. The invisible was visible before his eyes, and he could see the mantle, and he was made a citizen. *Bath qôl*, the daughter of the voice of God—it had spoken in his hearing, and he was moved to tears because he thought: *Somebody knows my name.*

This, as we said, is the end of the story.
The beginning and the middle follow.

2.

From the first days of my ministry at Grace—when I still wore massive, black-rimmed spectacles, unpolished shoes, unmatching clothes, and a halo—I took a greedy pleasure in the ritual of greeting members after worship, shaking the hands of every soul who'd sat to hear me preach.

There was one main door from the tiny sanctuary, through which all the people had to pass. Down some steps from that was the narthex, where I took my pastoral stand— and then, to my left, the double doors of the church, which opened outside to sidewalks and lawns and the weather.

"Good sermon, Reverent," parishioners complimented me. I grinned. I agreed.

"Glad to have a preacher not afraid of preaching!"

"Wonnerful, wonnerful."

"Very spiritual, Reverent."

"Well, I enjoyed myself today, that's a fact."

"Fellow pumpin' gas at the Mobil station, he said to me, 'Yeah, but can that white boy preach? I mean *preach?*' Well, I was proud to tell him, 'White or purple, my pastor gives as good as he gets, yessir.' I shut his mouth. I told him, 'He can raise the dust.' Amen, Reverent—right?"

"Right," I said.

"Right," said the grinning face in front of mine, one in the file of parishioners greeting me: "Just keep on doin' what you doin'. Right."

They were including me—on their own terms and in their own language embracing me. They were glad I was there, and I was glad to note their gladness. More than glad, I was relieved. Happy days, those early days! I had position and a host of admirers.

Well: the fact that the church was black, and the concomitant fact that it sat in the inner city, caused a sort of contention in me which needed this affirmation. Actually, two separate problems needed this balm in my breast.

First, I was purely flattered that a people not of my heritage received me as one of them and praised me in the reception. That spoke well, it seemed, of my deeper humanity and my ministry; it laid to rest the uncertainty I'd had of whether I might prove prejudiced or meanly provincial. Success in the city must be prized. So the problem of doubt was eased in a private rush of triumph—to God be the glory.

As for the second problem, I was (I explained to myself) inexperienced. I was (in actual fact) a stranger on this turf, untutored. The inner city was altogether foreign to me—and I might have been a pastor inside the church, with all the rights the office granted me; but on the street I was

alien, ignorant, an interloper notably white. I was (to put the
issue more plainly than I ever did in those days) scared.

But the more that the members of Grace affirmed me
here *and* on the streets, the safer might be my goings forth—
and even the inner city might be persuaded to accept my
pale, improvident presence.

Oh, love me, Grace. But love me out loud, okay?

I was hungry for handshakes in those days to calm my
fear. So much depended on their approval and their praise.

"I'm the kind of person," said Eleanor Rouse, "who brings
her flowers to the living. I don't wait till they're dead. So I
tell you to your face: Pastor, *my* Pastor," she said, "you got
my respect."

And Eleanor Rouse had my immediate, complete devotion—most especially because she, who had called me *her*
pastor, was not a member of Grace. She belonged to New
Hope Baptist Church, only sometimes attending our worship with her parents. Besides, Eleanor was a most outspo-
ken women and might therefore bruit my goodness abroad,
in the courts of the neighboring kingdoms, as it were.

She had a vigorous handshake. I returned it with equal
energy.

"To God," I said, "be the glory."

"Thank you, Jesus."

"Thank you, Eleanor—"

And then her mother, whom the people called Miz Lil,
followed in her turn; and then her father followed next,
both of them shorter than their daughter, shorter than all
their children, it turned out: shorter than most of the pop-
ulation. But a couple most serene. A couple, whom to meet
and know, was comforting indeed.

This Miz Lil distinguished herself from the common run
of compliments for several reasons. She looked me directly
and kindly in the eye, no embarrassment on her behalf, no
qualms regarding me. Her gazing caused a sort of solitude

around the two of us which lent her words importance. Nor did those words come tripping from her tongue. A fox eye had Miz Lillian, a canny glance, and a habit of pausing before she spoke. Her thoughts were parceled one by one and personal.

Under the aegis of such a spirit, one remembers what was said, yes, word for word. And one is a bit discomfited if he cannot fully interpret the oracle.

On a certain Sunday Miz Lillian said, "Well, you taught us today."

And then on another Sunday she fixed me with her eyes: "Hooo, Pastor," she said, "you preached today."

Her husband was another matter. Douglas Lander, always equable whatever the time of day or year, wherever the little man turned up, downtown or mowing the lawn of the church or shoveling snow, could talk at an endless length, his sweet voice on and on, his glasses bobbing up and down, his single, final, philosophic observation for any topic he could not otherwise resolve or explain or morally excuse being: "One o' them things." So he sang the tougher problems of life to rest and lived in peace in spite of them: "Just one o' them things." With such a metaphysic, the man was fearless; he could talk on anything, no subject too perilous for him.

But Miz Lil was chary of her words. She knew how she would end whatever she began. She gave infinite space to Douglas, undismayed however far his droning led him; but her own subjects she chose with a watchful care.

Therefore, I began to notice, Sunday after Sunday, that Miz Lil had but two words for my sermons. One was "teach," and one was "preach," and there surely was a difference between the two. But I could not, for all my pondering, guess what that difference was.

Everyone else in the congregation seemed at peace with Miz Lillian Lander, innocent of her effect; they seemed to take her much for granted—like children sporting on the shore of some almighty, rolling ocean.

Me she made nervous.

On a particular Sunday, then, when she reached to shake my hand, I held on and began to question her.

"Miz Lillian?" I said.

The fox eyes, sharp and kindly, gave me more than a moment, gave me the whole day if I wanted it. "Pastor?"

"Sometimes," I said, "you say I teach."

"Mmm?" she said.

"And sometimes you say I preach."

"Mmm-hmm." She said this high in her sinuses. She smiled. She waited.

"Well," I said, "is there a difference?"

The old lady raised an ironic eyebrow, as though she thought an educated seminarian would know of differences. But she kept on smiling. I felt suddenly brutish and lumbering in front of her. And white.

"Of course there is," she said.

"Well?" I said, making a smile myself, embarrassed. "What," I said, "is the difference?"

Now Miz Lillian was holding my hand in hers, which was work-hardened, her little finger fixed forever straight, unable to bend.

"When you teach," she said, instructing me, "I learn something for the day. I can take it home and, God willing, I can do it. But when you preach—" She lowered her voice and probed me the deeper with her eyes. "—God is here. And sometimes he's smiling," she said, "and sometimes he's frowning surely."

I grinned. Her language was elemental, but I chose immediately to take it all as a compliment, for the teaching and the preaching together—but for the preaching especially, which seemed to be the calling of the holy God into our little church. What a mystic power that gave my homiletics, like shining from shook foil! I grinned.

Miz Lillian Lander smiled and released my hand and went out the double doors.

But in the next instant Douglas Lander floated into view, shrugging as though in apology for his wife. He shook his head while he shook my hand. "Just one o' them things," he sang, seeming to ease some little friction, seeming to salve some little thorn between us—as though we men could stand the female nature which we couldn't understand. "Just one o' them things," he said, and I lost my grin.

In my hypersensitive state a prickle went up the back of my neck. Why would Douglas think he had to cover for his wife? What had I missed? How was Miz Lil's compliment one of Douglas's "Things"?

Or wasn't it a compliment at all?

What had the woman said to me, *of* me, truly?

Oh, the more desperate I was to make sense of it, the more foreign seemed to me the language of the inner city. Black talk: teach and preach! Black talk: smilin', frownin'. What exactly did I *do* to make it teaching, or how was I different to make it preaching? *Yeah, but can that white boy preach? I mean PREACH?* What did she mean by "God is here"?

Maybe (I mused alone in my tiny study) I am not, at the bottom of it all, a part of this people. How can I know, if I don't know what I do to them? Maybe Miz Lil is the only honest one among them, though she speaks in riddles. Maybe I'm the dupe of a harmless, necessary deception: because they need some sort of pastor, they'll gladly make this pastor think they like him—*ack!*

And then came a Sunday of revelations. And then came the sermon in which I told a story to illustrate some point.

I don't remember the point. But I do, for two particular reasons, remember the story.

First, it was factual. I drew the story from personal experience in the church and in that inner city neighborhood, involving a woman who had been and gone before the telling of this tale. She was a transient. No one, I thought, would recognize her.

Second, when worship was over Miz Lil took my hand in the narthex, and held on, and gripped it until it hurt. She wouldn't let it go. She pierced me with her fox eye. "Pastor," she said softly, "you preached today. Pastor," she whispered in the solitude she caused around us, "God was in this place."

She said this with utter conviction. But the diminutive woman was not smiling. And she would not let me go. . . .

3.

(Herewith, an account of the experience, a portion of which was "preached" on the Sunday when Miz Lillian killed me with a word.)

Marie

All day long she sits in front of her shotgun house, in a cotton dress, on a tubular kitchen chair, gazing at nothing, rocking: the crazy lady, surrounded by a patch of weed she does not mow.

Neighborhood children call her the crazy lady because she mutters to herself. They sneak to the tree behind her; they watch her gesturing to the air; they hear her arguing with no one at all, and their eyes grow wide at the aberration. "Pastor! Look at the crazy lady!"

She does them no harm. She scarcely admits their existence. Perhaps she would deny the existence of any in her world except a few men, and those only of necessity.

One day I said hello to her. Well, that house is right across the street from my office, and I am a pastor, after all. "Hello!" I called with a friendly cheer. She froze midsentence. Her mouth snapped shut, her nostrils flared. She stared at me over her right shoulder. I came halfway across the street. "Hello," I said. "I'm the pastor here. We're neighbors, you see. What's your name?"

No answer.

Her body is a boiled bone, curved like a rib-bone, gaunt. Her eyes are huge, the dome of her head is huger. Her age is impossible to tell.

"What's your name?" I said.

No answer. The skull-gaze only, undecipherable. Which left me in an uncomfortable predicament: how to close a conversation that never started?

But a kid no more than two or three years old came ripping down the sidewalk on a wretched trike. "Marie!" he shrieked at the top of his lungs. "Marie! Yaw-waw-waw! Yaw-waw-waw!" He rocketed over the curb, lowered his head like the bull, and made directly for my suit pants. He wasn't pretending. At top speed this kid meant to run me down. "Yaw-waw-waw-waw!"

So I learned that her name is Marie, and this was her child—though she did nothing to stop him and merely watched me dodge his assault—and that was the last conversation we didn't have together.

And I learned to leave her alone. I could only wish that she left me alone as well.

This kid of hers is an affliction to Christian piety. Nobody disciplines him. Up and down the street he rides like a wandering siren. His mother disappears into her muttering, and no one's there. He shatters the air as though the city's afire. And no one is there. He's a disaster, an act of God, a tight tornado three feet high. But *I'm* there. My office is the tiny room to the right of the chancel, no windows, one outside door to the fire escape—to Gum Street. I am there. And I am forced to choose, when the kid is screaming, between two sacrifices: either I will shut the door and stifle in the still, hot air. Or else I'll open the door and pay for the breeze by enduring the noise of that boy. Either way I pay. Neither way is it easy for me to work in my study.

But I pity the kid. I do not blame him. I've heard him lift his voice in a truly wounded anguish, the poor child wailing in abandonment. I've looked and seen that his mother has locked him out of the house, and then his screaming doesn't frustrate me. It hurts me.

This is what happens: at sundown men begin to come to Marie's front door, alone, in pairs. They knock or they do not knock. They enter. Almost immediately her child is put out like the cat, and he whirls around and he beats on the door and he howls. Finally he sits on the stoop and gives himself over to the tears alone. Time those tears: twenty minutes. Then do not blame the boy.

The crazy lady across the street from Grace Lutheran Church, who lives in a haze the whole day through, who regards me with a rabid eye, who regards her baby not at all, is a prostitute.

So then, this is a serious question of ministry, of Christian and civic responsibility—of charity to the child, if nothing else: what should I do about Marie?

Well, it's a ticklish circumstance, isn't it? Rights and freedoms; contrasting lifestyles; morals, to be sure—but by what authority could I approach a woman who wouldn't talk to me? I'm new in the neighborhood.

I did nothing.

But Marie did something. And this is what happened between us.

One night I sat reading by a small lamp in my study, all the doors being locked to the church (for fear of the lurking inner city?—for safety, for common sense and safety, since the members warned me, "Lock the doors when you're alone"), all the lights being out in the church save mine. One night while I was reading at my desk, someone began to whistle inside the building.

I froze in my chair. A tingling tightened all my flesh. It has been my habit from childhood, when confronted with a fright, first to pretend that the fright's not there. To freeze in whatever position I had when I sensed my danger. But my heart goes ramming against my ribs, and my face may seem indifferent, but my ears are roaring.

Deep in the darkened building, smack in the middle of the inner city, far from any assistance I could in the moment imagine, someone had commenced a weird, a coldly passionless, whistling.

I prayed to God that it would stop. Just go away and release me.

It didn't.

I stole a glance into the sanctuary, to the back of the sanctuary, to the door that leads to the narthex and downstairs. No light. No one had switched on a friendly light. There was only the darkness made ghostly by shadow and shapes from the stained glass windows, effigies in glass.

Twice in the past year thieves had broken into the church. But no one else had been here at the time.

Why in God's name would a thief disclose himself by whistling?

Okay! Okay, I'm the pastor. I never figured that ministry meant law enforcement or fights or bloodshed or whatever was about to be required of me—martyrdom!—but I am in charge. The building is my responsibility. I'll see who you are (you idiot!) and what you're up to.

I crept from the warm light of my study into the sanctuary. I crept down the dark aisle toward the back. The floorboards creaked. I froze. And I found in the midst of my terror that I was angry. Furious, in fact, to be sucked into a confrontation I hadn't caused and didn't deserve. I hated this whistling thief.

But hatred wasn't enough to ease my fears. The whistling

was below my feet. In the basement. The nearer I crept to the steps downstairs, the more I swallowed. In the narthex, now, I heard it loud in ecclesiastical pits. In the boiler room, which was dark, dark.

Inhuman whistling! I began to notice that it never took a breath. One note, on and on and on—a mechanical sort of whistling.

I burst into the boiler room, crying, "Hey! Hey!" horrifying myself.

But there was not a soul in all the gloom.

And the whistling continued undisturbed. Above my head.

I reached up. I groped what I couldn't see. And touched pipes. Water pipes! Oh, my heart nearly flew in its happy freedom: water! How could I mistake it as anything else? The whistling was running water; the noise was water rushing through the plumbing of the church, ho ho! I could handle water.

Behold: I was bold again, though panting still from a host of emotions. And the conclusion to my private drama seemed clear and evident: find the faucet leaking water and shut it off. Ah.

I went into the men's bathroom right next to the boiler room. I checked the toilet, the sink, the urinal, and found all of them dry. I had almost turned to leave, when a shadow in the window caught my eye. Something outside. This window was at ground level facing the parking lot. I put my face to it—

Some*one* outside!

Lord, there was a thief here, after all.

Under the dusk-to-dawn light, crouched so close to the window that we might have kissed, but busy at the lawn faucet, unaware of me, filling plastic milk jugs with water from Grace Lutheran Church, was Marie.

I jumped backward. For two minutes I stood mute on the near side of the wall, listening to the water go, feeling her

presence altogether too close, feeling (instantly) abused, a
victim, a sucker. Apparently brick walls did not keep out the
corruption of the inner city. Marie was taking our water as
her due, no effort to ask us. Geez! the presumption griped
me. She was busy stealing. She was reaching into the very
heart of the building, even to frighten me in the privacy of
my study. I felt very, very vulnerable.

The whistling fluted up and stopped. She'd shut the water
off. When she passed the window, I saw her from the knees
down, lugging in each hand two plastic jugs of water, and
then I was alone again—and full of anguish.

I should do something about this, you know.

I went up into the sanctuary and switched on the lights
and began to pace up and down the aisle.

I had no idea what to do about Marie's little theft—or the
arrogance of it. Well, well, well: water isn't communion ware,
after all. What do you pay for water? Pennies. So let it go.
That's what I said to myself. Just let it go. And I thought:
if the city has turned off her water, you can bet they've
turned off her gas and electricity too. The woman's without
utilities. And she's got a kid who needs to drink and wash
and use the bathroom. So calm down and call it charity and
let it go.

Yeah, but that kid nagged at my mind. What was she
teaching her child? That he could take whatever he
needed—whatever he wanted, for heaven's sake. Any child,
I don't care who or whose it is, deserves better than this
poor kid was getting.

And then that's the next thing that nagged: what is the
ethic for supporting a prostitute, even by inaction and non-
involvement? This is a church, after all. We have a covenant
with virtue, after all, a discipline, a duty, a holy purpose, a
prophetic presence. Shouldn't I talk to the woman?

Precisely at that point all my abstract inquiry skidded
against reality. *Talk* with the woman? Why, the woman
doesn't talk! She stares you a moribund stare. She scorns

you with murderous scorn. Talk with the woman? I might as well reason with the moon or argue with the whirlwind. Who knew, if I truly approached her, whether she would flee or fly at me with a gun—or simply stare as though I were some dream that she was dreaming.

"So let it go." I said that out loud in the doorway of my study.

It didn't ease the itch of responsibility in me, fiscal responsibility (Grace pays for its water too, you know, and we have members no better off than this particular profligate), social responsibility (that kid stuck in my mind), moral responsibility, and even an evangelical responsibility. But nothing at seminary had prepared me for such a dilemma as this. I had no wise solution. I simply had no other solution at all.

"Forget it," I said and, as proof of putting the issue behind me, I went into my office, sat down in my chair, picked up the book I had been reading, and bit my lower lip. "It really doesn't matter. It isn't worth the worry. Let it go."

And so it was that I sat glowering at a page of print, in a church ablaze with electrical light, in an inner city that had bested me, at nearly midnight of the clock—when the whistling began all over again.

Sometimes when your neighbor does something to annoy you, you feel compelled to go and watch her do it. You know that you'll learn nothing new by looking. That's not why you need to look. You're angry, that's why. And anger wants to see its cause. Anger wants to get angrier. It is sweet to feel a just and righteous wrath—that's why.

So when the whistling began again I was out of my chair and down the aisle like a shot. I verily flew down the steps and into the basement, into the men's room, flew! I thrust my face to the window and looked into midnight and squinted to make my eyes adjust. I saw the figure beneath the street light. I saw the body bending at our faucet. Two feet from mine I saw a concentrating face—and I let out an astonished yip, and I leaped from the window.

That wasn't Marie. Four more milk jugs at his feet, thankless pomposity in his manner, a skullcap clutching his head—who was this drawing water from the bowels of Christendom? One of the prostitute's *johns!*

I tell you truly, doubt was gone in a flash. I knew straightway what I would do. I had a sudden vision of Grace Lutheran Church, the building itself, rolled over on her side like a helpless sow, while *all* the people of this neighborhood like wriggling piglets were pushing their snouts into her belly and sucking and sucking the poor church dry. "Nip it," I hissed with inspired clarity. "Nip it in the bud!"

I slipped into the boiler room, where the water was whistling one note over my head. I reached up to find the coldest pipe. I fingered along that pipe, feeling for a knob. Found that knob. Turned it to the left, and heard the whistling choke and stop, then covered my mouth and swallowed giggles of glee. For I saw in my mind's eye the john hunched over a faucet that suddenly died in front of him: drip, drip, and nothing.

I had shut the water off.

Even so in the end did a cleric and the church prevail, by cunning, not by confrontation, and no one was hurt, and no one's feelings or reputation was wounded, neither the church's nor the prostitute's. We could coexist on opposite sides of Gum Street. All in a rush of inspiration, a problem had been solved; and I drove homeward feeling equal to the task at hand, as sly as any rogue in the ghetto—a native. I slept very well that night.

To God be the glory. Amen.

4.

Down the steps and through the narthex, making agreeable racket with each other and greeting me one by one, the

members of Grace filed out of the church and into the daylight. Worship was over. I was shaking many hands.

I loved the ruckus. I loved the genial disorder. I was at
home.

"Pastor. Did that really happen?"

"It happened, Herman."

"Well, you just don't know 'bout some folks, do you?"

"No, no. You never know."

"Takes all kinds."

"All kinds. Say hello to Janey for me, will you? Tell her I
missed her."

The next man said, "Just one o' them things."

I almost laughed aloud. "One of them things, Douglas,"
I said. His observation struck me as perfectly accurate. He
slipped from view like trout in a stream, flashing silver at
the stem of his glasses.

"Pastor?" All at once, Miz Lillian Lander. She took my
hand and we exchanged a handshake, and I let go, but she
did not.

"Pastor?"

Her voice was both soft and civil. It was the sweetness of
it that pierced me. I think its tones reached me alone, so
that it produced a casement of silence around us, and the
rest of the people receded from my senses: there was Miz
Lil, gazing up at me. There was her shrewd eye, soft and
sorry.

"You preached today," she said, and I thought of our past
conversation. "God was in this place," she said, keeping my
hand in hers. I almost smiled for pride at the compliment.
But Miz Lil said, "He was not smiling." Neither was she. Nor
would she let me go.

She paused a while, searching my face. I couldn't think
of anything to say. I dropped my eyes. *God was in this place.*
Evidently she meant more than a spiritual feeling, a patting
of feet and gladness. The old woman spoke in velvet and
severity, and I began to be afraid.

"Her grandma's name was Alice Jackson," Miz Lil said staring steadily at me. "Come up from Kentucky and went to school with me, poor Alice did. She raised her babies, and then she had to raise grandbabies too. She did the best she could by them. But a body can only do so much. Pastor," said Miz Lil, "when you talk about skinny Marie, you think of her grandma. You think of Alice Jackson by name. You think to yourself, she died of tiredness—and then you won't be able to talk, except in pity."

I stood gaping at the floor, a large man with monstrous glasses on his face. My shoes were skinned at the toes. Look. Look around. Not another member wore such wretched shoes to worship. This was embarrassing. My whole face stung with the humiliation.

Miz Lil continued to press my hand with her large, work-hardened fingers, the little finger forever straight. She would not let me go.

"God was in your preaching," she whispered. "Did you hear him, Pastor? It was powerful. Powerful. You preach a mightier stroke than you know. Oh, God was bending his black brow down upon our little church today, and yesterday, and many a day before. Watching. 'Cause brother Jesus—he was in that child Marie, begging a drink of water from my pastor."

Miz Lillian Lander fell silent then. But she did not smile. And she would not let me go. For a lifetime, for a Sunday and a season the woman remained immovable. She held my hand in a steadfast grip, and she did not let it go.

4

One in a Velvet Gown

1.

On Halloween the fireman's wife came walking down the middle of Overhill Street, straight down the center of my street. She was white in the deepest dark. She was singing. Her voice was not lovely. It was shaking and high and old. Yet I caught my breath at the distant sound, which was like wind in the attic or wind in the branches at your window, a fitful, alien wind—and I peered at the floating, approaching figure.

I thought she was wearing the robes of a ghost. I had streaked my own face with charcoal and wore my father's shirt reversed. But she wore no costume at all. She was wearing a full-length slip, low on her shoulders, long at her ankles, and nothing more. She walked the concrete barefoot. Bare were her arms, naked her back to the weather. The shame of it astonished me. And when she passed in front of me I saw that neither was she singing. She was weeping. My heart and all the world fell silent at the passing of the fireman's wife. She moved in a terrible solitude.

"Jesus, Jesus," she was saying. It might have been a hymn. It might have been a nursery rhyme: "Jesus, the demons won't leave me alone."

Her knees kept punching the front of her slip, so that moonlight broke like water on the nylon. The braid of her hair swung like a censer behind her. In all my life, this was the first and the most lasting vision of the awful beauty wrought by human malice in the humans who endure it.

"Ring the bell," she chanted, "I don't care. Fill my house; no, I don't care. Crowd my bedroom. Gather and laugh. Poor Emily isn't there. No, Emily doesn't care, and Emily isn't there—no more, no more—"

Emily. Her name was Emily. I never knew.

Poor Emily. She was, she said, a realist. She didn't have an Alternative of Giants. She never had the consolation of the stories of the mind.

2.

My father taught me how to find my way to school. Late in the summer he put me into a wagon with my brother Paul, and then he pulled us all the way up Overhill Street—and a long way it was, too—until we came to a corner which he told me I must remember.

"See that stop sign?" he said.

I looked at it.

"Now, do you see that house on the corner? Can you remember the two pillars on the porch?"

I said that I could.

"Good," he said, "because here is where you'll make a left turn. Turn left, Wally. This is the only turn you have to remember. But the school is on the other side of the street, so you'll have to cross. Don't cross here. There's a stop light at the school. Cross there. I'll show you."

So then we turned and he pulled us down another street, block after block after block of pulling, and he showed me the stop light and the stripes on the concrete and the brick pile which was to be my school, surrounded by a chain-link fence.

My father was very careful in his instructions, anxious that I should understand them. I was going into the first grade. I was the oldest of his children. And it was appointed that I should walk by myself to school in the mornings, home again in the afternoons.

As long as I sat fork-legged in the wagon, with my little brother between my knees, I felt confident. And as far as the daily journey was concerned, when my father or my mother drove me in the car I managed it without distress.

But when I actually went forth on my own, this odyssey frightened me to tears. Dad said, "Wally, it's only a mile," and I didn't think he lied to me, but neither could I explain to him how treacherous and long that mile was, or what happened to me when I traveled it alone.

It was a mile of foreign territory. The faces I saw were not my people. None of them knew me. They looked on me like a criminal thing. They knew the laws of their lands, but I didn't. In order to get to school each day, I had to pass through valleys of the shadow, unconvinced that I would make it to the other side. I truly believed, each time I went forth, that I might die.

How could I tell my father that?

Or how could I explain to him what happened to my person on the way? I shrank. The farther I went from my own familiar neighborhood, the littler I became. The houses around me, they grew huger, they swelled to tremendous sizes. The distance from corner to corner expanded, because my legs diminished like rubber bands. So I would run faster and faster, my lunch box flying at my hand, but I kept arriving at corners later and later. The whole world seemed vast and pitiless, because I was reduced to a dashing dot with a lunch box. And that's how I imagined I would die: *pop!* By vanishing.

So how could I tell my father that? It was true, of course—but of course he wouldn't believe me.

So I pretended that my breakfast made me sick, and threw it up.

I cried whooping tears, true tears, no pretense at all.

I became recalcitrant, disobedient, tardy. Punishment plus a ride to school was infinitely preferable to walking alone into danger and to death.

But in the end I walked. And that is how I came to know the fireman's wife. Her house, two blocks up Overhill Street, became for me a refuge from the peril. It was by her kindness that I survived.

Until the days I walked to school, my neighborhood *was* the world; nor did I shrink in that place, though it wasn't without dangers itself, because I knew precisely how I fit in it. The people of Overhill Street, they knew me. Therefore I knew me too. I wasn't a big person, but I was a whole one; and what I was, the strengths and the weaknesses together, remained unchanged from day to day. I didn't have to pay attention to identity, then: just be, because I belonged. Such being is freedom, although it is caused by the strictures of being known and by a thoughtless obedience to community.

These are the blessings of familiarity: being and freedom and confidence.

So these are some of the people who granted me a place in the world and a self:

Ross. He lived across the street from my house. We were friends, though we never noticed it to talk about it. We had a fight once which lasted a long time, full of violence and fury, but which ended the instant one of us (I don't remember which of us) threw a punch. Pain was a shock which neither of us had anticipated. Ross's family owned the only TV in the neighborhood. I glanced at it once and saw my first actual death. I saw a close-up of a woman's face. A man was choking the breath out of her. Her eyes swelled and her tongue came out, and so did mine, and I mourned that woman several days, aghast that people could die. Ross's father had a car with a rumble seat instead of a trunk. He took us for rides.

Chipper and Laurie. They were a sister and brother who lived on the corner in the other direction from my school, and who had the remarkable gall to run from their mother when she wanted to spank them. Incredulous, I watched them hide beneath the dining room table. This was a liberty I'd never seen before: outright defiance! Their mother barked her shin on a chair and made a mighty uproar, but she never retrieved the mice from underneath the table. My mother would have cut that table in two. Chipper and Laurie were friendly kids. The world is full of wonders.

Jimmy Newman. Jimmy lived immediately next door. On the Fourth of July he produced a package of black pellets that looked like licorice, and told me he could turn them into worms. He lined them up on the brick of an outdoor barbecue, then lit them with matches. They hissed and extended into long, twisting shapes, exactly like agonized worms. Part of me believed absolutely that they were grey worms. Part of me thought them nothing but ash. But the two parts never argued inside of me, and I accepted both explanations as the truth. I said, "Where do they go after they're worms?" He answered gravely, "They turn into nails." And because he could show me nails—a rusty clutch of nails—in the bottom of the barbecue, I believed that too. The world is full of wonders, but this was not one of them. This I accepted as the natural way of things, a matter of fact.

Jimmy's grandmother came out one day and screamed at me because I was throwing bread crumbs in her yard. She was a short woman, swollen, angry. I thought I was feeding birds. She thought I was wasting food and causing trash. But then my mother came out and screamed at Jimmy's grandmother with a truly stunning arsenal of words, and so began a war which never ended. Jimmy and I didn't play together after that. But I mention this family because, despite the enmity, they were also people of my neighborhood and essential to its familiarity.

Clyde. In fact, Clyde was not from the neighborhood, nor

was he a friend of mine. He lived across the alley behind
our garage, in a house that faced an anonymous street.
Therefore he was something of an alien. But he roamed,
Clyde did. And his presence had a powerful, predatory effect. He must be mentioned.

In Clyde there always hummed the deep machinery of
violence. His pale, lashless, empty eyes, his emotionless
mouth—they were a lie. His easy, liquid stride and the sub-
duing murmur of his voice were all a lie. Clyde was blonde
and lean and three years older than I. And evil. The boy
could kill.

I had seen him—in my own garage when the car was gone
and the door left open to the alley—take by the tail a garter
snake as long as a cable. He raised this snake to the level of
his vision, holding his arm straight out. He walked from the
sunlight into the garage where I was, not a trace of feeling
in his face, and dangled the serpent between us. "Watch,"
he said. The snake kept trying to climb itself, as if its body
were a flagpole. Clyde gazed at me a while. I said nothing.
The instant the snake relaxed and let its head hang down,
Clyde doubled himself at the waist and with a terrible swing
of his full right arm snapped that snake like a whipcord—
then held it up again. "Watch," he said. The creature was
quivering. "Snake's blood is thick," Clyde told me, dead-
voiced. "Watch." The serpent's mouth had skewed sideways,
its bottom jaw loose like a flap of shoe leather. Clyde was
right. Soon, as slowly as syrup, a red drop rolled out onto
the bottom jaw and hung there till it was huge. Snakes don't
close their eyes when they die. They just keep looking at
things, frowning as if in criticism or displeasure. Neither did
Clyde close his eyes. But neither did he frown. There was
utterly nothing in his face, not pleasure, not displeasure.
Merely a pale gaze and murder.

But he was right about snake's blood. It is very thick. I
actually heard the red drop hit the concrete of my garage.
It sounded like a lump of boiled vegetable.

3.

She began to compliment, and I began to grin—

So I was running very fast one day. I was urging my legs to go as fast as they could go down the strange streets, when a woman made herself apparent on the sidewalk ahead of me. She was watching my approach. I was thinking that my neighborhood couldn't be far now, because my spirit was almost exhausted and I was so miserably tiny.

Maybe my smallness lent the woman strength.

For she said, "Do you know what this is?" and I stopped immediately, as though she had cried a command at me.

But she'd only just spoken it. "Do you know what this is?"

She had iron hair, like a helmet of hair, drawn back from her forehead and tied in a single, hanging braid—the way my grandmother tied her hair for sleeping. Her eyes were hooded with folds of old flesh, so that they seemed to be peering from animal dens. "Well?" she said. "Do you know?" She stood willowy erect, in a posture I would come to regard as Old World gracious; but her chest was caven. Her cotton dress was empty there. Her hands trembled. And glittering: the hooded eyes seemed glittering to me.

I shook my head.

"Child, you're a piece of work," she said.

I thought I might go on now. But her words had not dismissed me. The woman was watering her lawn. The hose wound lazily over the sidewalk like a snake.

"This." She tapped the nozzle, which made the softest wing of a water spray. "This." It was a nozzle as wide as a human smile, two score tiny jets, blameless threads of water. "Do you know what this is?"

I shook my head.

"Why," she grinned triumphantly, "it's a fireman's spout. Yes! My husband brought it home when he retired. He was a fireman. This is the genuine thing. Isn't that a pleasant diversion?"

I nodded.

"Yes, and he gave it to me. And he said I could show it to whomever I pleased." She paused, gazing at me. Evidently I was someone she pleased. I wanted to go home.

"Would you like to hold it?" she said. Her deep eyes glittered with eagerness. "This very spout has put out a hundred fires. Here, child. Here."

She coaxed the lunch box from my hand, then wrapped my fingers round the neck of the hose. "Like this," she said, still holding my wrist. Together we waved the soft caress of water over the lawn. "Good. Good. You are very good. My husband would have been proud of you."

Her hand trembled on my wrist. She smelled of soap. There was a blue vein working in her temple. She kept passing her fingers over her brow as though catching loose tendrils of hair; but there were none. Not a strand of hair was out of place. I really wanted to go home. A dribble of water down my left arm triggered in me the need to go potty.

"What is your name?"

"Walter Martin Wangerin, Capital six six four two oh."

"You go to school, don't you?"

I nodded.

"Yes. I knew you were a scholar. I've seen you serious. I watch you mornings and afternoons in passage to and fro. And there is your little lunch pail, of course. Observation with me is second nature. In my opinion," she said with a gracious sort of laugh, "Dupin was a very inferior fellow, and Lecoq was a bungler. I'm a realist, you know."

"I think I should go now, please," I said.

"Oh!" Her hand flew to her forehead. "To be sure! To be sure, you probably should!" She said this with such a sudden vigor that I feared I'd hurt her. "And I'm done. My little plot is probably drowned. Walter Martin," she said, and then she frowned, snatching invisible hairs at her forehead. "Please, is it Walter Martin?"

I nodded.

"Well, Walter Martin," she brightened, "I have very much enjoyed our conversation together. Who cuts your hair?"

"My dad."

"He does a very good job." She touched the cowlick on my skull. I was holding the hose alone by now. "Tell him for me, sir, that he is an excellent barber. Would you like a Tootsie Roll?"

I nodded.

"Do you smile, Walter Martin?"

I nodded again. And then I made a smile.

"Come. Come, let me shut the water off. No. I'll tell you what we'll do. You shut the water off. Here. Lay down my husband's spout right here. You shut the water off whilst I go get you Tootsie Rolls. We'll not waste time, all right? There. On the side of the house. The faucet, see? All right? Does that sound fine? All right."

Her hooded eyes flashed a sort of fever—so many things to do. She hastened up the little sidewalk by her house, pointed at the faucet as she passed it, then disappeared around the back. I put the nozzle down. It whispered messages to the grass. When I bent I felt a terrible, terrible urge to pee, so I pinched my mouth fiercely. I went to shut the water off.

Even while I was turning the knob, the fireman's wife reappeared beside me, smiling.

"Put out your hand, Walter Martin," she said. And then with great ceremony she counted three wrapped pieces of Tootsie Roll into my palm: "One and two and three. Perhaps you saw the hearse in front of my house this summer," she said.

Hearse. I knew that word.

Suddenly the fireman's wife bent down in front of me. "Why, what's the matter?" she asked, a true anxiety in her voice, her eyes searching mine.

I realized that I had groaned aloud, and I groaned again in spite of myself.

"Walter Martin!" Her eyes were instantly moist with pity and tears. "What's wrong?" She wanted to touch me, but she drew back. "Please. I'm sorry," she said, and I saw that she felt at fault for something. "What's the matter, child?"

I myself felt very embarrassed. But the situation had really grown desperate, and I was forced to speak.

"I have to go potty," I said.

"Potty?" she said.

"Pee!" I nearly cried it. "I think I'm peeing in my pants."

"Oh! Well! Yes, of course. And we can do something about that!" She straightened—erect, concerned, relieved, all at the same time. Smiling and serious. "Follow me, Walter Martin," she said, and she marched up the sidewalk, and I crept after the pendulum braid of hair.

All of the rooms of her house were very dark, except for the bathroom, the sink of which had been scrubbed so hard, I thought, that she'd worn the enamel to black metal in places. This room smelled overwhelmingly of the soap I'd scented on her skin. And beneath that there were old-people odors here, like the nightgowns of my grandmother. I did not feel alien in this place. I wasn't even conscious that I might have felt alien, though this was not my neighborhood. In fact, I was enormously relieved. And the fireman's wife was standing, she promised, guard outside the door.

This is what I sang while I peed: "Never laugh when the hearse goes by, for you may be the next to die. They put you in a wooden box, and cover you up with dirt and rocks." Soon I was bellowing it. I still sat down on the toilet, even to pee, and I took my time. "The worms crawl in, the worms crawl out—" This is a song that Ross had taught me. This is how I knew the word *hearse*. "You shrivel up and turn all green, and pus flows out like—"

The fireman's wife was subdued when I came out.

Silently she led me through a living room of darkness and imposing furniture and massive drapes. She opened the front door, and there was my lunch box on the sidewalk.

"Listen, Walter Martin," she said full seriously. "Any time you wish to use the fire-fighting spout, come visit me. Or any time you long for Tootsie Rolls, come visit me. Or if you like another kind of sweet, please tell me. I'll get it for you. The hearse was for my husband the fireman. Is the water tightly off? Are you consoled now, child?"

I nodded.

"Good. Good. I think you should go now too. Your parents will be waiting. But visit me. That was a real invitation. I am not much given to fantasies, you know. I am a realist. Ring my doorbell." She demonstrated, reaching around the doorjamb. As long as she pressed the button, a persistent ringing sounded within her house. I thought of a fire alarm. "Like that. Good-bye."

I walked down her steps to the front sidewalk. I picked up my lunch box.

"Walter Martin?" she called. She was still standing in the doorway. She swept her fingers past the hairline. "Good-bye?" It was a question.

I said, "Good-bye."

She looked old and formal in the door frame. Her shutters were painted green.

I gave Ross a Tootsie Roll that afternoon and chewed another in front of him.

He said, "Where did you get that?" He meant, Where did you get the money? Ross and I bought bottles of 7-Up with dimes, jawbreakers with pennies, Oh Henry bars with nickels. We found coins in the gutters of the street. We believed that certain gutters were luckier than others—like fishing holes. So he was asking me which lucky gutter had yielded up the money. He had no idea of the marvelous treasure I had discovered.

"From the fireman's wife," I said, grinning, rich with news.

And then I did the poor woman a grievous harm. I told

Ross of her grand promise to me. "Just ring the doorbell," I said. "She'll give you candy."

In the days and weeks that followed, Ross did. He rang her doorbell, and he earned Tootsie Rolls for his boldness. And besides that, he told her what other kinds of candy he liked.

So the news was spread abroad.

Chipper and Laurie traipsed from their far corner of the block up Overhill Street yet several blocks farther to the house of my friend and got candy for themselves. Behold: I had expanded the horizons of our neighborhood. Jimmy Newman rang her doorbell. Jimmy Newman ate candy. Everyone came to know of her, and everyone who rang the doorbell ate. But I was the only one who called her the fireman's wife. That piece of her history seemed totally irrelevant to the others. They all called her the candy lady.

Even Clyde learned of our vein of gold: Clyde, who prowled all neighborhoods with a silken, predatory stride; Clyde, whose house belonged in foreign territory, but who was not impressed by custom nor by boundaries or propriety—Clyde, the pale-eyed, rang her doorbell and received the candy he did not deserve.

And my brother Paul went and rang her doorbell when the rest of us were in school. He took advantage of his freedom, and he prospered.

But for me she was the fireman's wife, a genuine friend and a refuge. Her house became an outpost in the wilderness. Whenever I was rushing home from school, terrified of the perils of the unknown world, I set my mind upon that house and those green shutters. The image itself encouraged me.

No, the world between the school and my block had grown no kinder as the autumn grew cool. It was always dark with enmity and threat, and so long as I couldn't see the friendly houses, I was in danger. One false step could kill me. Watch for the stop sign, Wally! Watch for the porch with the pillars! Turn right and run! Run home!

Daily I shrank and prayed to Jesus to keep me alive. Daily, twice daily, I raced so fast, so dreadfully slowly past strangers who stared at me—

Wow!—look at that little boy go! But he has such a grim face.

Of course he has. That little boy is filled with fears of death. He doesn't want to die. But he doesn't think he's going to make it.

Just look at him run! Too bad he's a cripple.

Jesus, save me! Save me, Jesus!

Oh, how grateful I was when I saw the house of the fireman's wife ahead of me, her little porch, her green shutters, her promise of kindness and of candy. I swelled—literally. I jumped to my common six-year-old's size, and my breast was flooded with gladness. I giggled and dashed the last half block to her door, uncrippled and wholly able. I bounded up her steps and rang the doorbell, panting.

I'm here!

It's me!

I didn't die today, isn't that wonderful?

O Fireman's Wife, answer your door and look at me. Let me see the rope of your hair hang down, and let's have candy to celebrate survival.

By the first week in October, I had developed strong feelings for the woman. Perhaps she had in some ways taken the place of my Grandpa Storck.

4.

Cross patch, draw the latch, sit by the fire—

"Walter Martin?" The fireman's wife cracked her front door just an inch. I saw a hooded eye. "Is that you, Walter Martin?"

She never watered her lawn anymore, nor did we talk about the fire-fighting spout of her husband. Dry leaves were clutching her grass. The air had a bite. I wore a wind-breaker jacket.

"Yes, ma'am," I said, puffing and grinning at that single, glittering eye. "It's me."

"Because you are the person that I especially care to see, Walter Martin," she said through the door. "Do you understand that?"

"Yes, ma'am," I said.

"You've come for Hershey's chocolate, I expect?" she said. There was an odd, plaintive edge to her voice. I began to wonder whether she was in pajamas, if that was the reason she hid behind the door.

"Oh, it doesn't matter. Well, yes. Hershey's is good."

"And perhaps you'll want to sit a while?"

I nodded.

She began to pull the door open, nodding too. No, she was buttoned to the neck in a dress, not pajamas. And perhaps she had tied her hair rather tighter, since her eyes had a kind of staring appearance. "Because," she said, "I have a topic for our conversation today. I have something delicate to talk about, perhaps."

She led me into her living room, saying, "Walter Martin, I trust you above the other children." It was dark, severely draped. She said, "Won't you please to have a seat?" I sat on the edge of a large, uncomfortable chair and kicked my feet. With an unconscious grace—she always moved, it seemed to me, with an engaging loveliness and grace—she took a settee across from me. I thought to myself, *How odd:* from the outside her house seemed a little cottage trimmed in green. But from the inside the same house seemed a castle.

"No," she said, "no, that's not true. I trust you above all other people," she said. "That's what's true." She stood up. "May I rest your coat, Walter Martin?"

I had begun to unzip it. I shook my head. She sank to sitting again.

"Trust you," she said. "Therefore I can't. . . . Therefore I wish. . . ." Her fingers fluttered at nonexistent hairs on her forehead. "Oh, dear," she sighed. She smoothed the dress on her knee. "Well, first I'm going to tell you what my husband's name was," she said. "Did you want to eat the Hershey's chocolate now or later?"

"Oh, later," I said, smiling and swinging my legs. "I'm going to share it with my friend Ross."

"Ross?" she said in a voice suddenly faint, fixing her eyes on me.

"That's the name of my best friend."

"Ross? A boy? He lives nearby?"

I nodded.

All at once the fireman's wife exclaimed, "I'm out of candy, it's gone." She stared at me with a surprised expression, as though I had just said this, not her. And then, in a rush of words: "Yes, yes, you are a kind person, Walter Martin, to share your things with your little friends, and heaven knows I would rather die than blame the kindness in you. Does your father cut your hair with scissors? I only just assumed, you know. But I'm clean out of candy now, though I can't tell you why, it's a mystery, and I would appreciate it if you mentioned this new piece of information to him, to your friend—to Ross, to all of the other children," she said, and she gulped air, staring.

Into the silence that followed, I said, "No, but he uses a clippers."

"What?" whispered the fireman's wife, widening her eyes.

"My dad," I said.

I told her that my father cut my hair with a clippers, not scissors, two-handled clippers which had a hundred teeth and which pulled my hair when my father squeezed it. I truly liked to tell her such things. Her face lit up with an enthusiastic interest, and she obviously respected my wide knowledge of the world. Yes, I told her, he cut our hair in the basement. He would tie a bedsheet round my neck so tightly that my vision went pink.

"Pink?"

Yes, the whole world took a rosy hue, and I could see the veins in my eyes. They became a sort of lattice between my seeing and the basement wall. Once I fainted, with a roaring in my ears.

"Walter Martin!"

My father caught me. He has very strong arms. He has a work smell, a flesh scent which comforts me. He calls the haircuts crew cuts. We look like the backs of rabbits when he's done—

"Rabbits?"

"Rabbit-butts, round and furry."

The fireman's wife covered her mouth with the fingers of her right hand and began to laugh. I grinned back at her, vastly pleased with myself. Gazing at me, she laughed almost soundlessly till the tears filled up her eyes. I hadn't intended a joke, just an image. But if she perceived a joke in what I'd said, I wasn't about to argue. I was by nature a sober child. These moments when, by the luck of my language, I caused the fireman's wife to laugh—well, they were rare and wonderful indeed. Lo: in the presence of the fireman's wife I was that marvelous personage, a "character."

I said, "Rabbit-butts"—and together we went off into fits of sinful giggles, delighting in our libertine ways and in each other. O Fireman's Wife, you are a mortal angel, and I love you.

Suddenly a bell began to ring. We both jumped up, confused by the insistent ringing.

The bell kept screaming.

"Oh, dear. Oh, dear," she muttered, her fingers flying to her hairline. She was hesitating. I couldn't understand that. It took me only a second to realize that this was the doorbell, and then I thought that the next thing was, you answer the door. But the fireman's wife had a look of distraction in her eyes. Her iron hair seemed to be gripping her brain, paralyzing her. She wrung her hands. She forced herself to the front door. Just before she opened it, she turned to me and pleaded, "But I'm out of candy."

She opened the door.

The ringing stopped.

It was Clyde, pale-eyed on her porch, who immediately peered past her and saw me standing behind.

"Whatcha got, Wally?" he said.

I squirmed in a great discomfort, saying nothing.

The fireman's wife, still holding the door, said, "I'm clean out of any kind of candy, sir, and perhaps you will go away now." She'd lost her grace. She sounded fretful and old. The braid was Grandma's again, and this whole transfiguration wounded me.

"That's okay," said Clyde, leaning left and right to see me. "I'll take what Wally's got."

The woman whirled around and saw me and gave me an anxious look.

"You!" she said. Then she murmured, "No, um. No, no. No, Walter Martin shares enough. Um." She turned back and stared at Clyde. I didn't like Clyde at all. She said, "Wait." The vein in her temple worked like a crawling worm. She raised a hooked hand to Clyde. "Wait—just a moment, please," she said.

So then, I in the darkness and Clyde in a wide autumnal sunlight—we gazed at one another while the fireman's wife sank deeper into her house, sighing. I was hating Clyde then. He was lashless and impassive. She returned with five Hershey bars in her hand, each of them as civil as a Sunday suit. She gave them all to Clyde, then shut the door on him.

Instantly her fingers fluttered to her forehead. "Oh, dear, I forgot," she murmured. "I forgot to say good-bye to him." She opened the door, but Clyde had vanished. The porch was empty. "Something else too," she said, staring at the lawn and the fallen leaves. "What else did I forget? There were two things—"

Bewildered, tragically close to tears, she began to pull the door to, and then she noticed me. "That's you, Walter Martin! Oh, dear!"

I felt sad to be there. I felt so guilty Clyde had come. I looked around and reached for my windbreaker.

"That's right," said the fireman's wife. "You were about to leave, and here I am, shutting the door. Is that what I forgot? That you were going to leave?"

And then here was my lunch box in my hand. And I had my jacket on by now. But the fireman's wife still stood in the doorway so that I couldn't get by.

Suddenly she seized my one free hand in two of hers.

"Arden," she said.

Under their hoods her two eyes fairly smoldered with that word. Her look pleaded with me to understand that this was a very important word. "Arden, Walter Martin," she repeated. "The thing that I forgot. My husband the fireman, his name was Arden."

5.

Hark, hark! The dogs do bark. The beggars are coming to town—

Precious to me was the little green cottage at the end of my daily race. I rang her doorbell daily. But the fireman's wife was changing. The other children of the neighborhood still rang her doorbell too. But the fireman's wife was different.

She grew shrill. She said that she had no candy, no candy of any kind. Nevertheless, if someone hung long enough before her door—even after she had closed it—she would finally bring cookies instead. A lesser sweet. A sorry second to Tootsie Rolls to everyone's way of thinking, and soon even these came burned. But I didn't mind. I didn't blame her.

"I'm running out of cookies," she said, looking past me to the weather. "Maybe people shouldn't visit anymore. Maybe they shouldn't ring my doorbell anymore. Maybe they should just go away—"

But it truly wasn't sweets that brought me to her house. I had no easy way to tell the lady that I was feeling sad for her and yearned with all my heart for something to give her, some way to make her laugh, some words to comfort her poor, distracted, frightened, grandma's face.

"Can I go potty?" I said.

"Oh, well. Well, yes," she said. No joy. Worry, rather. "Come in."

And then, in mid-October, I did indeed have something to give her, a piece of wisdom nearly magical in power. It had rescued me from death. It could, I was convinced, save her as well. Surely it would delight her and cause her some moments of happy triumph—and she would praise me for the story I had to tell. She would raise her two hands up and laugh. *Oh, Walter Martin, you're such a character, sir. Bless my soul, I never would have considered the Giants on my own without your smartness—*

But this time when I rang her doorbell, she didn't answer. She didn't come to the door at all.

Consider the Giants:

Once upon a time a kid was running homeward with his chin tucked down and his lip stuck out and his grim eye on the sidewalk. Huffing and puffing was this kid, protecting himself from the evils around him by high speeds. He had made a right turn at a certain corner, and now the wind was in his face with dead leaves and malice. Well, with scowls of his own the kid was ignoring the wind.

He was thinking to himself, *Two more blocks to the fireman's wife. Two more blocks, home free.*

He had his fists in the pockets of his jacket, a lunch box under his arm.

At a certain distance past the turning-corner, the kid lifted

up his eyes and looked ahead—and then his legs continued
to pump, but his heart had almost stopped.

"Fireman's Wife," he whispered to himself, "where is your
house?"

He stared to the left and the right. He squinted ahead as
far as he could see. Dead trees and sidewalk. Nowhere—not
anywhere in his whole field of vision—was there a green
cottage or a single stick of familiar wood. But he had measured the mile in his mind no differently today than any
other day, and this was the end of it and that's where the
cottage ought to be, but it wasn't there.

"Three blocks?" said the kid. "Or maybe four?"

He ran with his eyes wide open now. The wind grew
colder and whistled and laughed in the trees and needled
his eyes to tears. All of the houses around him looked almost
like the houses of his neighborhood, but every one of them
was just a little different. No, this was not his neighborhood.
He was lost. He ran forward, getting loster and unhappier—
but he had done nothing wrong. He had turned exactly as
his father had taught him long ago. So the fact was, he could
not be lost. This was very bewildering. He ran and he panted
through his nose, and his stomach started to cry.

Crash! His lunch box slipped from his arm and hit the
concrete and jumped open. The waxed paper from his sand-
wich flew out and the wind tore it away. Used waxed paper
is a private thing, like underwear. The kid felt humiliated.
He squatted down below the alien houses, beneath their gazing windows, and he picked up his thermos bottle—but it
made a dry, rushing sound inside. The glass had shattered.
That was more than the kid could bear. Now his face began
to cry. He didn't even stand up again. He found that he had
run out of running. There was no more running in him.
And he wouldn't know where to run if he could. He said,
"I'm not lost!" He sobbed, "I'm supposed to be right here."

Still picking at his open lunch box, still holding the broken thermos in his hand, the kid cried out the terrible truth. "My neighborhood is lost!" he wailed.

And the cold wind screamed and howled, and the windows of the houses didn't even blink. The waxed paper had spiraled higher than the naked trees.

"It isn't funny," the kid whispered. "My neighborhood is gone."

Why it wasn't funny was, soon he would shrink away. He would disappear the same as the houses that should have been here. He felt the coldness creeping down his back, the locking of his joints in preparation for death.

"O Fireman's Wife, where did you go?"

All at once an absolutely unaccountable thing occurred. The waxed paper blew down from the sky and slapped the kid on the right side of his face.

Immediately he leaped up and cried, "All right! All right!" He made fists and a fierce face and he bellowed, "All right now, that's enough!"

Because the waxed paper in his face was *not* unaccountable—not if someone magical was teasing him. And that was the answer, of course, but he had been too dumb to see it before, so the Giants had had a good laugh, you can be sure of that.

The kid was shaking with anger. The anger felt very good to him, warm and empowering.

"I hate you, Giants!" he roared, turning left and right so that they couldn't miss the implications. "I hate you and I spit!" he cried. Free and proud, offended and angry at once, this kid reached down and shoved the thermos in his lunch box and slammed it shut and began to march back in the way that he had come.

Giants had played a trick on him. That's what had happened. Giants had picked up all the houses on his block and carried them probably one block over, then replaced them with dummy houses—just to frighten him. But if Giants had engaged in all that work to trouble a single kid, why, then this was a very important kid indeed.

He stumped in a magnificent wrath back to his turning-corner, glaring fury for the sake of any Giants still observing him.

"Wait'll I tell my mother what you did to my thermos bottle. Just wait."

When he reached the turning-corner he made an interesting discovery: this wasn't the right corner after all. He had turned one block too soon and had been on the wrong street all along. Ah, but that little detail was dismissable, no matter how true it might have been. Truer still, and not to be dismissed, were Giants of malevolent natures, mighty and huge and defeatable. Truest of all, endowing a kid with wizard powers of survival, was the hatred he experienced against those Giants. Both were real, of course: both his mistake and his rage. But rage felt infinitely more precious to him. He believed them both, but he valued the latter the more.

And why? Because the strength of his wrath would keep this kid from ever shrinking again.

So now he was racing in giddy hilarity down the next street one block over, his own full size and twice his strength.

Fireman's Wife! his happy heart was calling. Oh, let me tell you about the Giants! All you need, dear Fireman's Wife—the only thing you need to do—is to hate them!

Up the steps of the porch of the little green cottage Walter Martin flew. He beat on a ginger door. He knocked on a spearmint sash. He pushed a licorice button and made a bell weep deep in the halls of her castle.

She didn't come to the door.

She didn't answer.

Oh, but I had such a story to tell her. I had such a gift to give her—to save her from sadness and fear—that I kept my finger on the doorbell, saying, "Please, please," and

bouncing from foot to foot, repeating the story in my mind.
Once upon a time a kid was running homeward—

*Walter Martin, you are a character. You make me laugh and I
love you.*

"Fireman's Wife, please open the door—"

She never did. She never opened the door to me again.
And I began to worry that she had moved away.

In the days that followed, I suffered a sort of stomachache
that the fireman's wife had left the neighborhood without
first telling me—except that I saw her one more time. And
then that was the last time.

6.

The beggars are coming to town; some in rags, and some in jags—

There was a moon on Halloween, which could be seen
from my kitchen window even before the dark. A rising
moon. Paul and I streaked our faces in charcoal to give ourselves fantastical grace and grimaces. But he said he was a
pirate, and though we looked alike I said I was Sir Lancelot,
wearing my father's shirt reversed as armor. It came down
to my knees. I carried a double-barreled shotgun for protection. We each had pillowcases to gather candy in.

In an exciting darkness, then, we criss-crossed Overhill
house to house, ringing doorbells, knocking on doors, and
crying, "Trick or treat." The adults, with their living room
lights aglow behind them, would bend down and drop
wrapped candies into our pillowcases, smiling. The night was
cold and windless and busy with the black forms of children,
clutches of rushing children. No one was afraid.

Ross was sick.

Jimmy Newman said, "Knights of the Round Table have
swords, not guns."

I said, "Yeah, but this is real. It was my grandpa's before
he died."

"What difference does that make?"

Calmly I cracked the barrel of my shotgun, closed it, and discharged two loud bangs to prove it lethal. After that Jimmy Newman didn't argue anymore, and I really believed that the gun had been my grandpa's, because I couldn't think of any reason why it couldn't be true. I wasn't afraid.

"Grandpa used to shoot squirrels in the cemetery," I told Paul.

"I knew that," he said.

When the night grew very late, Paul and I ran over to Ross's house so that I could divide some of my candy with him. He was too sick to come to the door, so his mother told me what a terrifying costume I had, and I said that it wasn't pretend at all. She laughed and thanked me for peanut butter drops twisted in orange paper.

Mr. Ramsey was angry when we rang his doorbell. None of his lights were on, not the porch light, not even his living room light. He shouted that we had come a full week too late and we should check our calendars before we did such a stupid thing again. He slammed his door. He was an old man. I couldn't decide whether he actually meant what he said or whether he was tricking us without the smile. For just a moment, despite all the evidence to the contrary, I had the panicky thought that he might be right and that everyone else had participated in a communal mistake.

Paul said, "Shoot his windows, Wally."

And then we stood beneath a street light to check the candy in our pillowcases. The street light was a single naked bulb in a metal reflector suspended from crossed wires. It didn't illumine much. Rather, it made us surer of shadows. But we maneuvered our bags beneath it—smack in the middle of Overhill—in order to peer at the comparative sizes of our loads. So we were standing with our heads down when Clyde slid between us and stood staring at me.

Paul said, "Hey!"

"You're a liar," Clyde said to me. I looked up. He wore

no costume. My father's shirt, which hung to my knees, felt suddenly shameful on me. Under the dim light Clyde's eyes were hidden in skull's shadows. His hair gleamed like pewter. He stuck his chin at me and folded a fresh stick of gum into his mouth as though this were a gesture of contempt.

"You're a liar," he said.

"No, I'm not," I murmured, utterly ignorant of his meaning.

"Hey!" said Paul behind him. "I don't like you."

I said, "Shut up, Paul."

Clyde chewed with his mouth open, making a black gap in his face. Juicy Fruit. "You're a goddamn liar," he repeated, his voice silken, his breath pulpy with threat.

I said nothing. Overhill was empty save for us. Why was that?

"I told my brother about the candy lady," Clyde breathed, perceptibly pushing his white face closer to mine, and mine began to burn. "I told my older brother, Bring a truck. I said she's got a house full of candy, and he couldn't carry all the candy she's going to give him." Clyde bumped his chest against me. I stumbled backward.

Paul said, "Hey!"

"Paul, shut up," I warned him.

"On account of you," Clyde said, "I made my brother expect a haul. So you're the liar, not me."

"I never said nothing about a haul."

"So?" said Clyde, raising his eyebrows as if this were a new subject for conversation. His bloodless face peeled into surprise. "So, then—did you go to her house tonight?"

"No," I said softly.

"Oh? Why not?"

"Well. She's out of candy—"

"See? See?—you liar!"

Paul said, "I didn't go either."

I hissed, "Shut *up*, Paul!"

Clyde raised his right hand and placed it against my

cheek, which tingled underneath his palm. "Well, we went, Wally," he said. "We rang her doorbell, Wally. And the old bitch!—she never even came to the door. My brother said that I was a liar—"

Compulsively I pushed his hand away. "Don't," I said, and I saw immediately that I shouldn't have done that.

"Don't?" he whined. "Don't? Wally, did you say 'Don't'? Why not?"

"Because," I confessed, "I don't like you to touch me."

Clyde's face twisted. Black shadows knotted in his brow. He drew back his hand and slapped my cheek a stinging blow. "You like that better?"

"Shoot him, Wally!" Paul began to jump and down. "Take the shotgun, shoot him!"

"Paul, shut up!" I hissed, keeping my eyes on Clyde.

Clyde's face was smeared with rage. "You want to know what we do to people who cheat us?" he screamed.

"No," I whispered. I didn't.

But Clyde went on and screamed this silly thing which sounded savage in my ears.

"We gum them! We gum them!" he fairly shrieked. "We gum them, by God!"

He took the drooling wad of gum out of his mouth and stuck it on the knuckle of his right fist and drew back his arm, his face pure white with fury. I was standing dumb, my hands at my sides, the pillowcase in one, the shotgun in the other. Clyde spun his body and punched me in the stomach. I barked once, then doubled down and knelt on the street, squeaking, trying to get my breath. But I didn't let go the pillowcase or the gun.

"Mom! Mom!" Paul sounded a distant alarm, running away.

"Gum them, by God," Clyde repeated above me, where I couldn't see him. "Are you listening? We jammed gum in that old bitch's doorbell," he said. "And gum in the liar's belly."

There was a moment when absolutely nothing happened. My gut had gone into a spasm. I sweat and simply could not breathe, though I made a cave of my mouth. Clyde's shoes hung before my face, a mystery of patience.

"There, now," he said in a silken voice. "I feel much better." The shoes moved. Clyde walked away into the darkness.

My breath came back in shudders dangerously close to crying. And my eyes were swimming in tears. But I thought that Clyde might be around and I wasn't going to cry, so I made a hideous woofing sound and crawled on my knees to the side of the street, dragging a candy sack and a toy gun in either hand. I managed to sit on the curb.

All my senses were purged in that moment. I saw and heard the night with weird precision and perfect clarity. A mild breeze had begun to rock the street lamp on its wires, so all the little shadows were shaking their heads, and the metal reflector around the bulb was squeaking—chirping, it seemed to me, like a bird. The trees all down the street snaggled the breeze in a whispering sound. Somewhere somebody shut a door. A dog barked.

And then I heard singing far to my left. A night song, high, unnatural, a wandering soprano so lonely and so earnest that it tingled in my scalp. Soon this was the only sound I heard. As soft as it was, it filled the night. Dream-music.

And then a white shape gathered in the blackness a block away. And then it was a figure floating toward me as smoothly as the breeze. And the nearer it approached me, the more aware I was, and the quieter I grew with awe: this was the fireman's wife.

She was walking down the dead middle of the street with unspeakable grace. No spirit she. No ghost.

She was undressed! She wore nothing but a slip, and her shoulders were wasted. She was barefoot on the concrete street.

"Jesus, Jesus," she was singing, "the demons won't leave me alone."

No—but she wasn't singing either. When she passed beneath the yellow bulb, I saw with horror how her hooded eyes were streaming tears. My friend, my fireman's wife, was weeping. She was so old! Her forehead high, but the grandma's braid hung down her back, and the slip was only a slip, after all, and I felt so ashamed for her. Her flesh was as white as flour.

She didn't even see me sitting on the curb.

"Ring my doorbell; I don't care," she wept in a wretched voice. My body shivered to hear her. My face felt her presence as she passed by. "Fill my house; no, I don't care," she chanted. "Crowd my bedroom. Gather and laugh. Poor Emily isn't there." She continued down the street. In the direction of Chipper and Laurie's house. Diminishing. "No, Emily doesn't care. Poor Emily isn't there—no more, no more—"

Emily. Her name was Emily. I had never even thought of the fireman's wife as having a name. Emily.

It was hearing her say her name that broke me down. I bowed my head in my arms and started to cry, and then I couldn't stop. My stomach hurt so bad from Clyde. And the passage of the fireman's wife—Emily—had changed Overhill itself into an appalling place, a street as dangerous and unpredictable as nightmares. But she was no dream. She was no ghost. She was just more sad than any I had ever seen before, and solitary. Where did she think she was going?

I bawled into my arm. And this is the reason why I couldn't stop: I felt ashamed. I felt so guilty.

"Did he hurt you, Wally?"

This was my mother beside me on the street. I accepted her coming without surprise. I stood up and buried my face in her stomach and continued to cry.

She held me. "Did Clyde hurt you?" she said.

I shook my head, but I couldn't answer her. I just hung on.

"Wally? Wally?" she said, stroking my hair. These tears of mine were endless, bottomless. "Wally? Why are you crying?"

Because her doorbell is ringing right now, ringing in an empty house, and her name is Emily.

"Wally?" My mother grew anxious and tried to pluck me from her waist. "What's the matter? How can I help you if I don't know why you're crying?"

Because I am the one who told the other kids about her in the first place. Because there aren't any Giants in the world. There's Clyde. And there is me.

"Wally, for heaven's sake! If you can't get a hold of yourself, I'm going to say I have a baby on my hands—and his name is not Paul."

5

Robert

I was walking east on Gum Street through the sort of rain one ought to have anticipated. Morning had been cloudy; the clouds had bellied low above the buildings; but I had gone forth in a ministerial distraction which took no account of the weather.

Busy, busy: I had already met Helen Alexander on Eighth Street to plan a neighborhood association meeting; she was the president, I was one of two founders, we were concerned that our slice of the city should receive a fair portion of the Community Development Block Grant moneys which the federal government allocated for Evansville. We wanted media coverage to prick the conscience of the director of the Department of Metropolitan Development, so that he could neither deny, neglect, nor dismiss the inner city. Busy.

I had already visited two members of Grace in Welborn Hospital, had prayed before a surgery, had donned a green gown and a mask to sit in quarantine with a young woman whose eyeballs had turned as yellow as gold.

I had already walked over to West Chandler, had mounted stairs to the high, tiny apartment of Dana Varner, who required Communion and conversation. Old Dana, old blind eyes, the endless entrepreneur: his rooms fairly bristled with candles and tiny lanterns, samples of the merchandise he sold to—God knows whom. Dana had talked. I had sat in a pastoral patience, at once suffering and concealing the itch of my busyness.

Busy! But in charge. Eighth Street and Welborn and West Chandler were all in the same general vicinity. I had planned

the morning's circuit with admirable practicality in order not
to waste a minute on my own account. The rain had begun
to fall while I was in Dana's apartment. I strode, therefore,
the faster, coming eastward on Gum.

Busy, then; and in control of things—but walking nonetheless. I had resolved to walk the neighborhood as often as
possible, and not to drive through it encased in glass and
steel. "Hello, Miz Crowe," *sitting on your porch, rocking, nodding, waving back at me—wearing, I see, your workday wig, coal
black and functional:* "How are your ankles today?"

"They're fair, thank you, Reverend. They're swole, but
fair. I think I'll keep my money this go-round an' leave the
doctor alone."

"Glad to hear it. See you later, Miz Crowe."

"Later, Reverend."

Walking: in order to know the neighborhood. Walking: in
order to be known. Walking—although I admit it cost me
some peace in the beginning, for I grew tense among the
strangers and felt my difference when the children stared
at me. I still could not walk on Lincoln comfortably, where
the young hung out on the hill by the pool, where men stood
in knots by Doc's Liquor Store, their spirits feral, their deep
eyes veiled and watchful when I passed, like leopards on
rocks at the zoo. But I walked. I puzzled the city together
for myself, put people in their proper houses, connected
children with their mamas, smelled pork and cabbage in the
evening air, heard the thumping rhythm of music through
the walls, considered my station in this place, smiled at folks
and nodded and walked on.

I was a minister, wonderfully busy, truly in control—and
personally present.

Therefore (as I said) I was walking east on Gum through
a dreary rain toward Grace Church, when I caught sight of
a small man on my left, suffering a sort of apoplexy.

As quickly as I saw him, even so quickly did I snap my
eyes away from him.

I can be forgiven this dodge: it was Robert. I knew Robert. Robert was trying to hail me in the rain. This would take a while, and longer than I had.

The little man made half a wave, the wave cut short. Half a greeting, half a smile, half a thought—all of them chopped in the middle.

"—because, er, on account of," he was saying. "Say," he was saying: "say you, my man, my man—um—" He wiped his nose on his sleeve and waggled his head. He dipped his face and laughed soundlessly to himself about himself.

I sped up in the direction of the church. I hunched my shoulders and pinched busyness all over my face.

Well, it took true determination and most of the day for Robert to break through the mists that surrounded him. Robert was not a bad man. Just a space man. He lived on another planet. Better yet: he *was* another planet, a wandering globe that had slipped its orbit and swung too near the Earth and—to everyone's surprise, including his own— had taken up residence in a rental room on Gum Street east of the Lutheran church. He stood in his doorway now, a man of indeterminate age, mumbling and chuckling and struggling toward some sort of greeting.

I had almost reached his sidewalk. I was walking now at the speed of hurtle.

Generally one had warning when Robert drew near. Usually one could take precautions not to get caught in the field of his friendly gravity or sucked into his alcoholic atmosphere. *Tippy-tippy-tap-tap:* the little man carried a cane wherever he went, striking the ground with it. Sweet Robert!— it wasn't a cane at all. It was, in fact, an umbrella shaft from which he'd stripped the cloth and the metal ribs. It was a rod so skinny that I had often wondered what was the value of the thing, or what could it support. But *tippy-tippy-tap-tap*, it sounded fair warning; it gave one notice to close the office door, to bury one's face in a book, or else to leave before

Jack Daniels became a happy satellite to the rest of one's busy day.

Usually, I say, there was warning. But this time I was walking and vulnerable.

And this time, before I'd gained the safety of the church, gentleman Robert produced an explosion so startling that I stumbled, stopped, and stared at him.

" 'S'HAPPENIN'!" the short man boomed. Birds flew up from the eaves of his house. Robert jumped backward and blinked and then beamed, as though he'd shot a cannon he didn't know he had. And I stood gaping at him—and that was all the weakness that he needed.

"Reverent!" he roared. He'd entered the common world. "Here, Reverent! C'm'ere! Come see what I got. I got sumpin to show you."

I was caught. I was wet. I had no umbrella. Robert's umbrella had no earthly purpose nor protection against the rain. I was the Reverent, obliged to my office and to righteousness. Therefore I was caught and could not decline the space man's invitation into his dry room.

"C'm in." Robert stood back from the door as straight as the bishop of a chessboard, blinking raindrops from his lashes and beaming. "C'm in."

The room was Stygian. It smelled sweet with sweat and with sleeping. All the walls were close. There was a bedframe and a mattress, with one scrawl of a cover on it. There was a wooden chair at a wooden table, a weary hot plate, an aluminum pan with kernels of corn in it, an ancient porcelain sink on two legs, attached to the wall—and under the sink, a cardboard box.

Robert followed me in, took a deep breath, exhaled miasma, and hung his twitch of a cane on a hook on the wall.

"Rest your coat?" he grinned.

I had no coat.

He didn't notice. He rubbed his hands beside me with a slow, most glowing satisfaction. "Awright," he said. "Aw *right!*" He gazed around his room with a beaming, proprietary pride. "Okay, then. Awright."

Two roaches from opposite sides of the wooden table met at the hot plate to discuss dinner.

"Robert?" I said. "You wanted to show me something."

"Isn't that wonnerful, Reverent?" he said with a beaming appeal.

What? What was wonderful?

Suddenly the small man sank down to the floor in front of me. On his knees he shuffled toward the sink. Grunting, then, he pulled the cardboard box out into dim light, pushed it toward my feet, and stood up again.

The box was full of things. Things. Mason jars, a cordless radio, bicycle spokes, aluminum cans, plastic cigarette lighters, a trivet with two legs. Things.

Robert hitched his belt, straightened his neck, then threw his left arm wide in a magnificent flourish, gesturing toward the cardboard box. "Reverent!" he declared, "anything. Anything."

I looked at his box of things and didn't move.

Perhaps he interpreted my confusion as modesty, a hesitation which he, the host, should straightway overcome. He put on a brighter smile. "No, but anything you want," he said, "she's yours." He began some serious nodding of his head now. "Y'all he'ped me in my need," he said, "an' now I wanna thank you. Reverent, I been thinkin' on this a long time, yes. I'm the kinda person pays his dues, and I owe you sumpin." Once more he repeated the expansive gesture, sweeping his arm toward the treasures, and beaming like the sun. "Anything," he said. His chin went up and his eyelids drooped. "Anything."

At last I understood.

For reasons that need no mention here (urgent, personal, ethical reasons) we had established a social ministry at Grace through which the hungry were fed, the destitute were given money for rent and utilities, children were clothed, mothers with dependent children were trained in cooking and budgeting—the poor were supported. We called it The Mission of Grace, and by it discovered levels of human existence we hadn't known before, subterranean souls unlike the stable, Lutheran community of our congregation. We were essentially a healthy people. These were in need. We had a mission. They came in marvelous numbers, once they learned of our goods and our goodwill.

And floating among them from deep space and dreams of his own remembered galaxies, had been Robert.

I bowed my head and smiled a pastoral smile.

"Robert, Robert," I said, "you don't have to give us anything. We do what we do for the love of God, not for payment in exchange." I spoke with a crisp articulation. I felt relieved, now that I knew what the man had in mind, for I could handle this matter. I could lay it quickly to rest and be gone. I was busy. I had business to do.

"How could we call ourselves Christian," I said, "if we turned our ministry into a commercial enterprise? All that we give is free to you precisely because it is the Lord's." What would I do with a two-legged trivet anyway? I patted Robert on the shoulder. His grin was sticking, but his eyes had become unmoored. It was working. I was in control again. "Ah, Robert," I said, moving toward the door, "you owe us nothing at all, no, not a thing. But I thank you all the same for the thought. That in itself is enough. And you know, don't you, that we're always there whenever you need our help in the future—"

I left. I chose rain to trivets. I dashed for my office, to everything left to do that day.

But on the following Sunday it became apparent that I had also left the matter uncompleted, that I had left the little man still groping through the mists for another way to thank us. And he did. Sweet Robert did, in fact, hit upon an excellent method of thanksgiving, a method sure to satisfy his honor and our religion, both.

Ten minutes before the service that Sunday I robed myself in the same white alb that I had used now, Sunday after Sunday and forever. I tucked a long green stole beneath the hood at the back of my neck and hung it down the front of me and caught it in the cincture. My head was bowed; I took the opportunity to pray: O Lord God, dear Father in heaven, I am indeed unworthy of the office and ministry in which I am to make known thy glory—

My shoes were new. Behold the gloss. They shone like the sun, my shoes.

Before leaving my study—one more minute yet alone—I glanced at the bulletin and marked pages in my hymnal so that both the order of worship and the hymns of the day would be right to hand when I needed them. *Alles in Ordnung.*

I was nervous, but not uncertain. I always felt nervous before worship. Well, people depended on me, and people would scrutinize me, so there was a sort of stage fright in the waiting; and God was here, after all, and that's another kind of scrutiny altogether. I preached without notes. That's risky. On the other hand, I was practiced in leading worship; I had a certain dramatic flair which seemed to please the people—and I was Lutheran. We were all Lutheran. And Lutherans, unlike looser traditions, have a very clear rubric to follow, a controlling ritual which comforted me; and I was in charge. Therefore I could be both nervous and not uncertain. I knew what was coming. No surprises. Amen.

I went out into the sanctuary. Faces, faces, murmuring faces, mostly black. The back pews were filled and so (happy day!) were the middle pews. The only spaces left were down front. Just twenty pews in this little sanctuary. Back and front were not far from one another. Even if the people sat toward the back, they were never far from me.

The murmuring softened toward a decorous silence. I stepped up into the chancel. There was a stained-glass Jesus above our altar, kneeling at his Gethsemanian stone, his nose, his brow, his cool composure all Teutonic. Black may have been the predominant color of our parishioners; but our mood and the prevailing discipline were Lutheran. Everything was done in order and good taste.

"In the name of the Father," I said, "and of the Son, and of the Holy Spirit."

The people, standing, said, "Amen."

I said, "Almighty God, to whom all hearts are open, all desires known, and from whom no secrets are hid: cleanse the thoughts of our hearts—"

And so the worship had begun.

We made common confession of our sins ("—have sinned against you in thought, word, and deed—").

We sang (where the rubric said in red, *The Entrance Hymn is sung*) a hymn.

We intoned the Kyrie, prayed the Collect, allowed a little space for announcements, read the Scripture lessons, sang another hymn. We rose at the *Stand*, we sat at the *Sit*, we honored the *Silence*. We were devout. We were holy, reverential, and devout—and I was not nervous anymore because, as Sunday after Sunday, worship was traveling smoothly. Oh, I loved this trustworthy people, and I, thank Heaven, was in charge of everything.

Nor did I forget my sermon.

I stood in the aisle between the two front pews and hitched my cincture and began to preach. I delivered an introduction of comprehensive clarity, touched upon the outline that would follow, launched myself into the first of three subtopics—and I preached.

The people nodded. I responded. I warmed to my subject. I lifted my voice. I lifted my eyes to the distances, and saw—

—Robert.

Standing squarely at the back of the aisle, his bumbershoot cane held grandly at his side, his hair picked out so that it stood upon his head in two high peaks, his clothing clean, his coat Goodwill but clean, a shocked expression on his face as though he could scarcely believe the wonderful thing he had done—was Robert.

Oh, the man looked vastly pleased with himself. He had contrived a way to thank us, after all: he had come to church. For what would gratify a Christian better than another body in the pew, another sinner saved? He came offering himself.

Robert. The little man cast greetings left and right by the nodding of his head, the tilting of those tall twin towers of hair. He beamed on people. And finding no seats in the back of the room, he turned his attention forward, toward me, blinking, smiling, and *tippy-tippy-tap-tap:* coming.

But I kept right on preaching. Subtopic two.

We nearly touched, so close did Robert come to me. But he spied a space for himself, the second pew from the front, immediately on my left; and he excused and grunted and nodded his way into that space. He sat. He lay his cane down on the floor, crossed his arms upon his chest, aimed a face of sweet benevolence in my direction, and prepared to hear some preaching.

Me, I just kept on preaching. Points three and four of subtopic two. Something of the wind had gone out of me. I labored more than sailed right now. But I could be dogged, and I didn't forget the sermon. I commenced an illustration for point four in subtopic two. I preached.

Midway through that illustration there arose a mild commotion on my left, second pew from the front. Robert had closed his innocent eyes. But Robert had begun to rock.

Now, I will admit that when I'm straining I tend to raise my voice, that sometimes I overcompensate with a forced, dramatic vigor. This could be dangerous, if someone is inclined to react more to the noise than to the instruction. It is possible that Robert was getting the wrong idea.

Therefore I softened my voice. I modulated my rhetoric. I whispered, but I kept on preaching.

And Robert kept on rocking.

I felt the prickle of sweat in my armpits.

Subtopic three.

By this time Robert's head was low and swinging, side to side. He was lifting a foot and replacing it, lifting the other, replacing it. He was patting his knee with his right hand. There was a rhythm in Robert I didn't recognize. It wasn't from my sermon, Lord. No, not from mine. Robert had another sermon going in his head—and that one wasn't Lutheran.

I kept on, kept on preaching, willing the people to listen to me, forbidding them to glance at Robert, and nearly squeaking when they did.

Up and down those twin peaks of hair went waving. Blissful was the look on his face. And then, in the midst of it all, he began that threatful Baptist practice—clapping.

I raised my voice in spite of myself.

Robert began to stomp.

I sweat. I raced my words. I drove my words with a hoarse command. The end of the sermon was in sight.

But suddenly Robert threw his two arms into the air and shouted at the top of his lungs: "I'M GOING TO PRAY!"

I stopped cold, staring at him.

Robert too was stunned. His eyes flew open. He seemed astonished by this spontaneous promise of prayer.

We were frozen, the two of us, waiting.

But then an angelic expression flooded his features, a radiance, as though he were overwhelmed by the pure, supernal beauty of his promise, and he nodded assent, and he roared it forth the second time: "Yep! I'm going to pray!"

Panic gave me a tongue. *"ROBERT!"* I cried, *"DON'T!"*

But wonder kept him deaf. "Yessir, yessir," he sang, his eyes beginning to droop, his nostrils swelling, all his breathing pumping toward a prayer, his arms beginning to tremble above his head—"Yessir, I'm going to pray."

I leaped at the man. I flew at him and grabbed his shoulders, one in either hand. "Robert," I cried directly into his face with a desperate authority, "you *can't* pray!"

He looked at me. "Why not?" he said.

"Because," I said, and I scrambled for reasons; dear Jesus, I needed a reason eyeball-to-eyeball with Robert. "Because," I said, "we have a *time* to pray."

Silence descended. A frown began to muddle Robert's brow. The angel-light grew dim in his eye, and by slow degrees his arms came down. "A *time* to pray?" Robert whispered. Evidently he had never in all his life been presented with such a concept before. "A time? To pray?" The little man deflated. The little man grew small again.

By inspiration of the Holy Ghost, I'd pushed the proper button. I was in charge again. "Yes," I whispered, counselor to counselee in private discussion together, "a time to pray."

"Oh," said Robert.

Carefully I backed away from Robert, as carefully as parents depart the nursery after persuading their children to sleep. Carefully I gathered up my little pieces of Lutheran sermon. Gingerly I preached. Subtopic three: conclusions.

Ah, me. And while I preached I suffered another commotion on my left, two pews from the front. Robert was apologizing for his error.

"Sorry," he mumbled to people on his right, "sorry," to people on his left. He dipped his ridiculous towers of hair to the people behind him. "Sorry," he hissed, "I didn't know y'all had a *time* to pray."

And so my sermon ended.

I crept back into the chancel. I sat. I opened the hymnal because the rubric said in red, *The hymn of the day is sung*. We sang a hymn.

My alb, I noticed, smelled mightily of sweat. But the serene Jesus in our stained glass window didn't sweat to pray. I noticed that too.

At the appointed time I rose and went to the altar and faced that Jesus and reached for the two collection plates, one in either hand. I turned, then, to the congregation, expecting to see two ushers who would take the plates from me—

—but discovered Robert instead.

He was standing squarely at the foot of the chancel, his hair ascendant like the spires of a cathedral, his posture erect, his face subdued, and in his right hand the cane which was really an umbrella shaft and nothing more.

Again we experienced a moment of silence together. And again he broke it.

"Naw," he said, shaking his head. "Naw, I ain' gome pray for you no more."

For me? That was the plan? For me?

Then he saw that I was holding the collection plates between us.

Were it not true, I would find the following detail too melodramatic to record. But I am bound to the truth.

Robert went fishing in his coat pocket and pulled out a dollar bill as soft as a handkerchief and dropped it in the collection plate, then turned and betook himself down the aisle and turned again and left the church.

Tippy-tippy-tap-tap, gone.

That cane! What could such a cane support, the denuded shaft of an old umbrella? Dignity. And prayer, I suppose. It had carried the supplication meant for me away from me.

Ah, Robert—what do I want with your money?

6

Miss Augustine

I used to cause myself sweats and panics by my daydreams, by the power of my imagination alone.

I would imagine that I was crouching on a high mountain ledge, on some lonely lip of stone projecting from sheer rock, the distance all dizzy below me and nothing above me to climb. I would, in the daydream, creep to the edge, peer over, and then begin to shake with fear. The height itself was not the problem, however high, however real I made it. *I* was the problem. For heights could always excite in me a perverse and nearly uncontrollable urge to jump; and I sincerely believed that if I relaxed my vigilance a whit, the wilder nature would prevail: I would leap, and I would fall. I would destroy myself.

Therefore even in my daydreams, I crept backward clutching at the ground; I curled with my face to the solid rock and shut my eyes and shut my ears—for the very air would murmur with a thousand sullen voices, "Come. Come. Jump." And my own spirit would answer, "What if—?" and "Why not—?"

So I would waken suddenly in the third grade classroom, trembling and sweating and hoping that nobody noticed the change in me.

Well, there was a certain reality to my daydreams, and there was good reason to doubt that I could resist temptation. I had at least once thrown my body into the blue air and had cracked my arm because of a moment's insanity.

Listen: this is how a boy can destroy himself:

I was swinging in a park in Grand Forks, North Dakota.

My entire school had scattered through the park, enjoying a picnic; so there must have been other children around, but I wasn't aware of their presence at the time. I was engaged in a private test of speeds.

The swing had long links, longer than my forearm, and a frame more lofty than any I had ever seen before. I had pumped myself to a remarkable height, forking my feet to the treetops forward, staring straight down on the earth at the backswing, ripping the wind between. I was hurtling so hard and so high that the chains went slack at my extensions, and my buttocks lifted from the seat. I made me go a giddy speed.

From nowhere—from the perversity inside myself—the thought occurred: *What if you let go?* It came as simply as that, in precisely those words. *What if you let go?*

I answered that craziness with honest sense. Right clearly I thought: *I'd hurt myself.*

But I let go anyway.

Rising on the backswing, I simply slipped from the chains and continued to sail higher than the seat itself, watching it tilt without me. Backward, upward, my body stretched straight in the air, and I saw the perfect sky, I saw the blue sky pure, and all my muscles loosened like water, my knees and my fingers filled with floating. I was a balloon. My feet rose into view. I thought: *This is how God feels, touching nothing at all!* Then my legs clocked over my head, and I was staring at the ground, and all at once a massive hand was pushing on my back. It thrust me down with increasing force, with astonishing speed to the earth, so the impact came before I could consider it. I hit and barked and lay still. There was no pain at first, only a dullish saturation, a sense of weight in all my bones. In fact, I felt no sharper pain until the principal had driven me home and I met my father and told him that I had broken my arm. Then it hurt, and then I cried.

But the real instruction of that experience was that I was

not to be trusted. There was an evil streak in my nature, and on a high ledge (so I imagined it over and over) against all sense and righteousness, I would probably jump.

It's a dangerous world.

The principal's name was Mr. Affeldt. He visited our house often in the year I attended Immanuel Lutheran School, because my father was the pastor of Immanuel Lutheran Church. They were colleagues with much to talk about.

Mr. Affeldt's ears grew so flat to the sides of his head that I used to consider he had walrus ears. He carried a pouch of flesh beneath his chin, and he smiled by the lifting of his top lip only, revealing a fence of long incisors. So the comparison to a walrus was complete, it seemed to me, except that he was not a fat man. He breathed like a fat man, rather. Through his nose. Even when he was smiling.

Of all the teachers at Immanuel, only Mr. Affeldt occupied an office of his own. Books rose up the walls of this room to the very ceiling, so that you had the sense, when you entered it, of entering the mind of Mr. Affeldt himself—each book a thought, each thought a silent eye inspecting you. To be surrounded thus by the cogitations of Mr. Affeldt (he was a man of cool rationality and legendary intelligence) could factor a child right out of existence.

On the books behind his desk (or else hanging from a hook when it was not in use), he kept a flat piece of wood, varnished and shapen with a handle, and burned across the face of it with the words: *The Board of Education.* I realized that these words constituted some sort of joke, because he lifted his lip when he spoke them and he showed his teeth. So I would shuffle my feet at such times and produce a knowing chuckle. But the joke seemed a bit joyless to me, since he used the wood to administer discipline to a student's open palm, or perhaps to a bending bottom.

Discipline. Regulations. The consequences of transgression. Nothing was hidden in those days. Nothing was particularly complicated. Principals and parents and teachers were not cryptic or tricky, but forthright and trustworthy. "Do this," they said, "and this will happen. Don't do this and the other thing will happen surely." And it did. It always did. They kept their promises. The world was orderly indeed, if a little severe. I knew what The Board of Education was for.

Miss Augustine, on the other hand, was mercy in my world; and I could abide the harshness of the whole world bravely for the sake of my third grade teacher, my Miss Augustine.

Early in the school year she had said, "Don't laugh in class. Please don't disturb the other children when I'm teaching them." It was a reasonable request, since she had to divide her time among three grades, all in the same room, and since at any given moment two-thirds of the students were working on their own. It was also a very persuasive plea, because Miss Augustine herself was a woman inclined to laugh—a pink-faced, musical laughter that stirred my soul when I heard it, a nearly killing benediction when I myself was the cause of that flush of delight in her face for something I had said—a persuasive plea, I say, because she controlled her laughter. She set us a good example. If she could get down to brass tacks, well, so could we.

So I said, "Hush!" to Corky Zimbrick, who sat behind me, and I tried manfully to ignore him.

Corky insisted on whispering jokes in my ear. I didn't understand that. I presumed that every student felt the same dear loyalty that I did toward Miss Augustine.

She had shoulder bones that hunched forward in a cotton dress when she stood by a student's desk. It was like the gentle revelation of internal vulnerability; lithesome and lovely were her shoulders' wings, vouchsafing through the fabric of her dress how tender the private woman was, entrusting me with secrets. And then I could hardly stand their fragility when in winter she pulled a shawl around her shoulders.

"Hush!" I hissed to Corky Zimbrick, not turning in my seat.

But Corky had a hasty manner of speech, a stuttering, breathless delivery that made all his words, however prosaic, nervous and hilarious.

"Ta-ta-ta-ta-ta-ta," he fired the words in my ear as through a peashooter.

That tickled me. I began to frown.

He said, "Shadrach, Meshach, and to-bed-we-go."

I chewed on giggles, like chewing on jujubes.

Corky put his mouth right behind my ear and caught me off guard with an obscenity: "Wally's favorite salad," he said. "Lettuce, turnip, and pea."

I let out a whoop. I said, "Haw!"

So Miss Augustine turned from the blackboard and gave me a look of such wounded disappointment that all my mirth turned sour inside of me.

I wanted, all at once, to cry for hurting her. No, no, but my station in this classroom was to protect her, not to distress her. My face burned with an earnest, genuine repentance.

And Miss Augustine deciphered my soul, I think. She was truly the mercy in my legalistic world. She said nothing at all, but drew the soft shawl tighter round her shoulders and turned to the blackboard again. My eyes lingered on her neck. My spirit swelled with gratitude. She hadn't reprimanded me.

One day I rose up in class and told a lie. I didn't recognize it as a lie—not until the following weekend. It was a story, rather, of sudden, astonishing power. I silenced a roomful of students in telling it; I encoiled Miss Augustine in the filaments of my own imagination, and I caused her almost to cry. Oh, what a wonderful gift I had! And how I relished the use of it.

Kathy Drees had just been telling us about the funeral of her aunt. She had described the open casket and the corpse and the weird chill that the corpse had left on her fingers when she touched it.

"Cold," Kathy said in a low and thrilling voice.

"You mean you actually touched her?" someone said.

Kathy lifted three fingers on her right hand to show us the frostbites. "So cold I felt it all night long," she said. "So cold I can feel it now." I was moved by the immediacy of her memory. Kathy had a nose like a little rubber ball, a plain sweetness about her that made the death seem cruel indeed.

But I was chiefly impressed by the effect the detail had on the faces around me: they gaped. And Miss Augustine positively melted toward this child who had touched with her own three fingers a corpse.

Well, sir. I could do better than that.

And instinctively I perceived the efficacy of two things: the corpse must be personal to me in order to be real for my listeners (but I couldn't use an aunt, since Kathy had taken that); and the story must bristle with detail. Miss Augustine needed to *see* what I would say in order to be cut by it.

So I stood up by my desk, and I said, "Miss Augustine, it was my sister."

She looked quizzically at me. Sharpen that detail.

"It was," I said, "my *older* sister." Give her a name. "Valery," I said.

I thought at first that I'd let this Valery die in infancy; but I would play no real part in such a story, and the purpose was to excite some sympathy on my own behalf. Therefore Valery was five years old in a twinkling. I was four. She wore thick glasses and walked with a limp. We lived on Overhill Street in Chicago, Illinois.

"She went downtown on a bus one day—"

Amend that. "*We* went downtown together on the Addison Avenue bus," I said. "We didn't get off until it made a big circle and came back to our street again—"

"Wally?" Miss Augustine interrupted with gentle caution. "Really? Would your mother have let you travel alone?"

"Oh yes," I said.

It was a reasonable doubt, I suppose; but my answer was honest. My mother had, in fact, sent Paul and me, not Valery and me, downtown on the bus on a Sunday afternoon; and then it had been me, not Valery, hit by the car. But I had bounced unbroken twelve feet from the bumper. Not Valery. Poor Valery!

"She ran round in front of the bus without looking," I said. "As soon as she was in the street, she stopped and turned. She was going to run back to the sidewalk, but—" Oh, lucky detail! "—Valery limped, you see. A purple car came roaring down the street and hit her—"

"Ah!' " said Miss Augustine.

"—and she rolled and she rolled. And the man that hit her had four daughters in the car. He jumped out and ran to Valery and picked her up, and Valery's arm was hanging down, so I started home to get our mother. I ran home all by myself. I was crying."

Miss Augustine covered her mouth and whispered, "I'm so sorry," her eyes beseeching me. I was creating something wonderful. The whole class sat stock still. Oh, I was flying. I wanted never to quit so sweet a flight of pleasure. Miss Augustine, I have touched your heart!

Detail by detail, then, I carried the class to the funeral, not unlike the funeral of Kathy's aunt; but my funeral contained an incident more terrible than the mere touching of the corpse.

"When everyone was looking at Valery in the coffin," I said, "my grandpa whispered that her hair and her finger-nails would keep on growing forever—"

"What?" said Corky Zimbrick, appalled.

"But Mom said, 'She's your sister, Wally. You should say good-bye to her.' So we went right up to the coffin, my mom and me, and I said, 'Good-bye, Valery,' because dying is saying good-bye, you see, and my mom, she started to cry. And then she said, 'Wally, you should kiss her.' That's what she said. She said, 'Wally, give your sister a kiss.' So I leaned over the coffin, like this. And I put my lips on her forehead, like this. And I kissed her. Now that," I declared to the classroom, "was cold. *Cold!* Valery was colder than ice. Valery was colder than winter. My lips stayed frozen for six days after that. I couldn't smile on account of, my lips were so cold."

I sat down.

Nobody said a thing.

Miss Augustine was devastated. She had made a prayer of her hands and was holding them at her mouth, gazing and gazing at me, speechless. Her tender eyes were swimming, and her face was pink with feeling, and I was proud. She loved me. I was a sorcerer. I had caused my teacher almost to cry. Miss Augustine, I'll be kind to you.

"Wally," she whispered, "how tragic for your mother."

Mr. Affeldt sat in our living room looking straight at me, his ears so flat that I couldn't see them. Miss Augustine had come with him. She was wearing a print dress with a collar that covered the back of her neck. She wasn't looking at me. So my face was stinging because the principal was, and my teacher was not, looking at me.

Actually they had come to visit my mother. They had spent some fifteen minutes alone with her—and only then invited me to join them. I had accepted the invitation right happily, but no one was smiling at my entrance, and my mother had said, "Sit down."

Miss Augustine kept her head bowed. I couldn't tease so

much as a glance out of her, and I wondered if they were blaming her for something.

My mother said, "Mr. Affeldt came to comfort me, Wally. Do you know why?"

I said that I didn't. My mother seemed very strong to me, hardly in need of comforting.

"Well, he thought it would help me if I knew," she said, "that my tragedy is known, that the church stands beside me, that I don't have to keep it a secret any more. Do you know what that secret might be, Wally?" she asked.

I shook my head. I knew so little of adult affairs.

"That I had a daughter," my mother said, "who died four years ago—"

Oh. My face began to sting, my chest to pant. Oh.

"—a grief so grievous," my mother continued, staring at me, while Mr. Affeldt kept his cold gaze on me too, "a guilt so deep that I shut it away and confessed it to no one. I made your father promise not to mention it. So I would never have known forgiveness for neglecting my daughter unless my son had let the secret slip. I am supposed to thank you, Wally," my mother said, "because Mr. Affeldt realized that he should come to speak the grace of God to me. Wally?"

"What."

"Should I thank you?"

No matter how pleadingly I looked at Miss Augustine, she would not raise her face nor return the look. Her flesh was drained white, her slender fingers folded in her lap. My teacher was ashamed of me. I had hurt her. I had told a lie too terrible for mercy.

"Should I thank you, Wally?" my mother repeated.

I shook my head. All of my words had fled me, and now I didn't look at Miss Augustine either. The knowledge rose in a heat around my ears that I was a very guilty thing.

"I think it's fortunate that your principal is here," said my mother, "and your teacher too. Now no one can doubt that the rules of this house are the same as the rules of the school—the same as the commandments of God, Wally. Mr. Affeldt knows that I won't abide a liar. He knows he has permission to punish you if you lie again. *Behold, how great a matter a little fire kindleth! The tongue is afire; the tongue is afire.* Do we all understand that, Wally?"

My face was a perfect fire.

But I was not going to cry. It was horrible enough that Miss Augustine should see what a sinner I was. I would not add to that an abject humiliation. I did not cry.

"Do we all understand that?"

I nodded.

I didn't move when everyone exchanged amenities and left. I was grateful to Miss Augustine that she didn't say good-bye to me, because a word from her might have broken my resolve. I might have wept.

For all his joking in class, Corky Zimbrick was not especially bold. That became apparent when I began to run the schoolyard with a gang of boys at recess: Corky wouldn't. The louder we got, the more he chose to stay in the classroom, he and a handful of girls, Kathy Drees, Lorna Kemble, and a tiny kid named Abner.

Well, and we did more than run the schoolyard. We galloped. We were a black-hearted gang of reprobates who galloped exactly like horses, slapping our thighs and crying, "Giddyup!" and charging the girls on the monkey bars, mocking them, befouling them with names and nasty language before we galloped around the corner: "Hi ho Silver, away!"

I took it for granted, given the changes I found myself making now, that Miss Augustine would reserve her tenderer expressions for someone else. And she did. But I hadn't anticipated that she would shower so much kindness on so many others so constantly. What had been mine seemed given indiscriminately to everyone—smiles and blushings, the murmurous music of her voice, the awful rounding of her shoulders—to absolutely everyone else. Well, so what? I broke pencil points when I wrote at my desk. So what?

And then the news circulated through the school that Miss Augustine was engaged to be married, and that the man intended was Kathy Drees's older brother, a farmer's son. I knew him. Neat hair; pure white temples; a pure white slash for a part; and for a nose, a rubber ball. So what? So gallop the harder at recess and slap my thigh and holler the louder, "Giddyup!" I hated Kathy's brother.

So what? So there came the time that Mr. Affeldt called the lot of us into his office after recess. Seven or eight sweating boys, we stood surrounded by his juridical books and listened to his imperturbably nasal voice and watched him talk by the lifting of his top lip only. When he began to refer to The Board of Education, I felt my bowels turn into water. But Glen Larson dissolved so quickly into wet sobs, and other boys began so shamelessly to wipe their eyes with the heels of their hands, that I stiffened myself and determined not to drop a tear—and didn't. Mr. Affeldt did not use The Board of Education that day. Rather, he lapsed into silence, a watchful, blinkless silence; and then he dismissed us by the merest nod of his head.

While the others were trooping out, he rose and approached me and dropped a hand on my shoulder. "Walter Junior," he said, "this is your last chance. Do we understand each other?"

And then it was that, in the park and urging my swing the higher and higher, I broke my arm.

I lay on the ground a while, aware of my bones and the sick shock inside my chest. My right arm didn't want to hang when I stood. It wanted cradling. So I carried it in my left hand to Mr. Affeldt, where he sat on a picnic bench in sunlight.

"I think I broke my arm," I said.

He twitched his eyebrows up, examined both my face and the protected arm, then stopped looking at me and led me to his car. He drove me home in a business silence. I kept my face impassive. When I stood in the doorway and saw my father coming toward me through the house, I lost control and I cried. But I kept my right arm to myself.

The doctor called it a green tree break. He distinguished that from a compound fracture, which he described in purple detail while fitting a metal plate beneath my wrist and wrapping it tight.

"Boxing?" he said. This was meant to be a joke. "Fisticuffs?"

"Flying," I said.

So then—what did I get for my rash behavior, my flight halfway to God? A half day home from school. I got a sling for my arm that tied behind my neck. I got assurances from my mother that we would visit an optometrist, though I truly did not understand the connection. I got a flurry of fame when I returned to school the following morning. I got permission to skip phys. ed., together with the command to stay in the classroom during recess.

But these were just candies. What was precious beyond expression, what I got when the recess commenced, was an opportunity I couldn't have planned because I could never have imagined it. I flew again. I flew the third time. And twice I was beloved.

Corky Zimbrick touched my sling and said, "What happened?"

With scarcely a thought to the answer, I said, "I flew."

"You what?"

"Flew."

Corky put on his comic face. "Ta-ta-ta-ta," he said. "Wally, Wally," he chuckled.

That I had said it, and then that he had laughed at it, filled my throat with a thick conviction. "I flew, Corky," I said. Lorna Kemble was in the classroom. So was the tiny kid named Abner. And Kathy Drees, all of us at the back of room for recess. "Kathy," I said, "didn't you see me? Didn't you see me fly?"

Good Kathy Drees of the bauble nose and the wonderful, guttural voice said, "Yes." She corroborated what I said: "You flew."

"See?" I said. "Listen, Corky, I pumped the swing," I said. "I pumped and I pushed and I pulled the swing, so high and higher. You'd think I could circle the top like a bucket of water and not fall out—that's how high I went."

Kathy Drees was nodding. She was watching me, but the flash in her eye was seeing my swing. "It's true," she whispered. I grew excited.

"Corky, Kathy saw it," I said. "At the very highest of the backswing, I just let go. I just let go, and I sailed into the air. I went out backward, and I spread my arms, and I was staring into the sky, and I flew. I was flying on a soft wind, and looking so high, so high—that I saw God!"

Now Corky Zimbrick was gaping at me. Kathy's eyes were shining a marvelous credence. Lorna and Abner were drawn into the circle. Oh, the sorcery was in me again, sweet, sweet, and the story was very true: in the classroom, on the wing of my words, I was gone again, flying.

Miss Augustine walked into the room and set a stack of books on her desk.

"The reason you don't see God from the ground," I said, "is God is big! Bigger than the sky. And the sky is huge and blue, and the sky is full of clouds, but even the sky is smaller than the eye of God. The sky," I whispered, "is a tear in God's eye, Kathy!"

Miss Augustine had begun to watch me.

Kathy's face was tipped toward me in speechless reverence.

Corky wasn't laughing.

I was king. I began to pant.

"The air makes a shelf in heaven," I said. "You slide that shelf like a slicky-slide," I said. "Airplanes find it and fly and they never flap their wings," I said. "And God said, 'I'll show you that shelf.' God showed me that shelf, and I turned on my belly, and I flew. I soared. I sliced the wind with my arms stretched out, and I looped the loop, and I saw the earth—" I was laughing now, because I was flying. "—I saw the park, and I saw the people, and I saw you there like dots on the grass—"

"Wally!"

"—but Kathy, but Kathy, but God forgot to show me the edge of the shelf, and I slipped right over it—"

"Wally!" This was Miss Augustine. I shot her a glance, and I saw at once that her face was a flaming pink, and my heart exploded with joy, because it had happened again: she was listening, and she loved me. She loved me! She admired the wonderful things that I had done!

"—slipped right over the edge of the shelf," I said with a frantic intensity. "Down I fell, and down in a dive, oh, down so fast that the wind was screaming in my ears, oh yes! I saw the ground, I saw it coming, saw you see me falling down—"

"Wally!" said Miss Augustine. "Stop it!"

"No!" I shouted, panting. "Wait!" I cried. "Wait till I get to the ending," I said—because then she would have such sympathy for me that she would hug me maybe and love me forever. I knew what was coming. She didn't.

"Walter Wangerin—" she whispered, but I raced on.

"I saw everyone," I shouted in the classroom. "The whole school, Kathy and Corky and everyone, and I said, 'I'll miss them all! Won't hit a soul!' And I aimed my body to the empty spaces, falling like a cannonball—"

"Stop that! *Stop that!*" Miss Augustine shrieked. She shrieked it and thumped the desk, and she looked—frightened. I think she looked—

All at once I didn't know what she looked like or what was happening.

Miss Augustine rounded her desk and began to march in my direction glaring at me.

But I couldn't stop. I couldn't stop. I was falling, and I couldn't stop.

"I hit the ground," I cried, staring back at her and rushing the words in order to finish. "I hit so hard I made a hole, and I heard my arm go crack! Crack! It was a compound fracture," I yelled. "The bone, you see, it pierced through my skin—"

In that same instant I realized that my ending wasn't working. Miss Augustine came bearing down on me, her face aflame. There was no sympathy in her face. And still, and still—though burdened with the knowledge of an unspeakable loss—I could not stop.

I lifted my right arm and murmured miserably. "The bone poked through the skin as sharp as a knife, you see, and the blood poured down my elbow too, and I hurt so bad, but I didn't cry, no I never—"

Miss Augustine seized my shoulder and gave it a violent pinch. I put my face down. But I finished my story. "Cried," I said.

"What's the matter?" said Kathy Drees. She was looking back and forth between the both of us. "What's the matter?" she said.

She was pleading her question, in fact, because she was sincerely confused, and I noticed that her chin had started to tremble.

"What's the matter?"

I felt sorry for Kathy. I knew what the matter was. And I wanted with all my heart to be good. I mean, I would have confessed on the spot. I would not have denied, but would have confessed that I had told another lie, a monstrous lie. That was the matter, that was the dreadfulness here.

But without a word Miss Augustine had already yanked

my shirt at the neck, the collar and the sling together, so I couldn't say anything at all. She pulled me out of the classroom, and we went walking down the corridor.

Miss Augustine didn't talk to me. She let me go and folded her arms across her chest. She hunched her beautiful, terrible shoulder bones, and drew the shawl so tightly closed that the knit stretched open and showed the print of her cotton dress. I could hardly stand those innocent holes of revelation. I stumbled to keep up with her. Her poor face was mottled sick with the redness. I knew what the matter was. She didn't love me anymore. It wasn't her fault.

It was worse than a lie, of course. I was not ignorant of the truth. In me there was the deep streak of evil, a perversity so villainous and so indifferent to precious, delicate things that it destroyed them—and I simply couldn't control it. Miss Augustine didn't love me anymore. She would never love me again. And this was not her fault. It was mine. No, I was not to be trusted: on a high ledge, even on the cliff of a stone-cold truth, I would probably jump and destroy myself.

It's a dangerous, mutinous world.

"Walter—"

Miss Augustine stopped walking. I froze with my face down, but my heart began to strain the leash on the chance she was about to change her mind and speak a merciful word, would reverse the direction my sin deserved, might love me again.

"Walter—" she said. Oh, her voice in that moment was a music of a thousand incipient vows. I waited, willing myself neither to move nor to cry. But if she intended some further word beyond my name, I never heard it.

I heard instead the rush of her shawl, and her knock on the principal's door.

It is an exacting world.

7

Baglady

I said into the microphone: *Robert contrived a frightening way to thank us—*

The sound system was good. It didn't echo back at me, though the building was, to my eye, huge, and the walls were far away. I held the mike in my right hand, walked a dais three steps high, drew the loops of electrical wire behind me, and swallowed prodigiously. If I got stage fright preaching in tiny Grace, what would I get in this place? Cataplexy.

I said into the microphone: *Robert decided to come to church—*

The people before me were smiling. Interested and smiling. No one meant me any harm. Yet these people were strangers to me, and they numbered—what? In the hundreds, all lifting their faces, leaning left and right in order to see me.

I swallowed and said into the microphone: *On Sunday morning, bang at the back of the aisle, the little man appeared—*

On the other hand, they weren't strangers truly. They were Americans at worship—no cause for nervousness. Evangelical, nonliturgical, unfanatical, calm and kind and self-possessed, a rational middle mix not even denominated, these smiling people offered me no threat—unless vast latitude and limitless, uncritical goodwill threaten the ortho-Lutheran because he isn't used to so much freedom, because he has to fill it.

I coughed into my left hand. I swallowed and spoke into the microphone: *Sweet Robert stood directly opposite me,* I said, *his hair picked out to double peaks upon his head, a shocked expression on his face, the thin umbrella cane held formal by his side—*

The smiles near me grew broader and heads in the distance nodded. Yes, they said, they could imagine my Robert. Yes, they recognized the irony of the situation and were ready to identify with me. Go on. They liked a story too. Go on.

I began to relax. And I went on.

Well, he couldn't see a seat in the back of the church, I said. *Grace may be little, but Grace ain't provincial. We got big-city ways—we fill the back pews first. So Robert commenced to walk the aisle in my direction—*

"Ha, ha," said the people.

Ah, laughter. I was grateful to these people. I hit a stride, and I went on.

This was the LaSalle Street Church, a congregation in downtown Chicago which I had heard about even before they invited me to come and preach to them. Our ministries were not dissimilar, though theirs was large, sophisticated, and far outstripped the infant Mission of Grace. They had an honest reputation for service. Well—and the territory they served was in itself notorious. Perhaps nowhere else in the country do poverty and great wealth neighbor each other so closely in such extremes.

The riots of the 1960s destroyed whole blocks of the near north side of Chicago in flames; but then the city regenerated itself by building modern structures on the land the poor demolished. Someone had been an opportunist, I thought when I saw the tailored fortresses. Some wealthy someone had reasoned with himself: "If the poor despise it, I will buy it. If the vulgar burn it, I can build." Some wealthy entrepreneurial someone constructed condominiums, impassive, impressive, impregnable in sight of the LaSalle Street Church.

But if you step outside the church and look left, you will also see a nearly unspeakable stacking of poverty: Cabrini Green, high-rise housing, warehousing, the desperate housing of the poor. Down the faces of these grim buildings is a dark, interior cleft, as though Vulcan had slashed each one from the hairline to the jawline with his hammer. But the architect did that. The architect caused this indentation as though some part of every floor in the building should be revealed to the world. "Is it nothing to you, all ye that pass by? Behold and see—" My heart recoiled when I saw that visible shaft. I felt ashamed, partly because I felt as well a fascination and watched for inhabitants to appear in the crack as a boy might watch for ants in an ant farm. I felt embarrassed for the multitudinous poor and for this society which solves them like a problem in structural engineering. Or maybe all my feelings and reflections came from shock at the scale of poverty. I knew the name Cabrini Green. But who knew it was so big, so big? And from this vantage, so globally silent? I was looking at the moon come down and grounded on the earth. I was, I guess, awakening.

And there across the way from me, when I stood on the church steps, rose those stony condominiums, each a mute, blank solipsism; but people lived there too. The contrast was monstrous. People and people, absolutely sundered from one another. I was a baby, waking.

Yet this consoled me: that another people altogether, these of the LaSalle Street Church, had turned their attention and their resources to the poor. They stocked and dispensed food with a practiced efficiency I could learn from; I could take their system back to Grace. They cared for the elderly. They knew about the houseless. With several other churches ("networking"—a new word for me), they supervised a clean, safe dwelling place for black and white together, for those financially dependent and those independent, for the young and the old.

And though they lived in other places through Chicago, though they were themselves a generally middle class collection, the rational middle mix, their language sounded familiar in my ears, and I was inclined to say "We" in the midst of them. "We are engaged in the same kind of ministry, aren't—we? And isn't that encouraging?"

I thought I would tell them of my experience with Robert. It would communicate our common bond: "See? I am your brother, even in Evansville." It might also serve as a sort of warning, in which I was the bad example: "If we grow cumbered about much serving, we might lose a willing humility and lose a world of good besides. Look what I lost in Robert." A cautionary tale, I thought. A sad one because of my fear and my foolishness. But an urgent one because it had been true and Robert, in fact, continued to live on Gum Street close to Grace. I still saw the little man pass on the sidewalk, though he'd never come back to worship with us, and I kept a guilty distance from his tapping cane.

Finally, my story might be some consolation to anyone at the LaSalle Street Church who had grown weary in well-doing: "See how near God is unto you? Angels do sometimes come in the form of the most oppressed. God is here. God is in Cabrini Green, and sometimes he's frowning, but sometimes he's smiling, surely."

They had asked me to preach to them. This is what I intended to preach.

So I was walking in a wide chancel, and the sun was shining in the windows, and a genial sea of faces bubbled and smiled at me, and I had begun to feel a homiletic confidence. No, this congregation need not be a threat or strange to me. See how they understood the story I was telling them?

I said into the microphone: *Robert spied himself a seat two pews from the front on my left-hand side, and he sat, and he laid his ridiculous cane on the floor—*

Even the children locked sight on me and blessed me with attention. I paused and permitted the tiniest twinkle in my eye: the next part of the story would be funny, a joke on myself. The people would laugh.

I said: *Somewhere in my sermon there arose a mild commotion on my left, the second pew from the front.* I affected a look of Lutheran anguish, and I said: *Robert had begun to—*

At that very instant, at the back doors of the LaSalle Street Church, there occurred a real commotion. Three people rushed in a bunch together and exchanged a hissing of words sharp enough that I looked up, even while I continued the story:

—Robert had begun to rock, I said. *He was lifting his feet and putting them down. He was patting his leg with his hand,* I said. *His eyes were closed. He was hearing some sermon with wonderful rhythm, but it wasn't mine, and it wasn't—*

Lutheran, I was going to say. And people, grinning wide as rakes, were waiting for me to say it.

But the hissing at the back of the church had suddenly stopped. An usher had turned in my direction looking woeful and helpless, while in front of the usher, as bright-eyed, pointed, and determined as a weasel, was a woman beetling forward at a frowning clip.

An old woman; a woman crook-backed, hunched at her shoulders so that her face thrust forward; a woman behatted, but the hat just sat on her hair, because the hair shot out around her head in a white and spiky nimbus, stiff hair, angry hair, hair capable of stabbing. This woman's face was full of the mumble of words. Her mouth was working words as though they were gum. Her eyes were darting left and right, pew to pew as she approached. What was she doing? With a draining horror I understood: the woman was looking for a seat!

The LaSalle Street people filled the back pews first.

"Dear God," I breathed, "who's doing this to me?"

The woman was clutching the handles of a shopping bag in two hands at her stomach. A baglady.

For the flash of a moment I was furious. This was altogether too perfect to be accidental. She was too classic to be true. She was an actress; this was a joke on my Robert story, but a baglady instead of a drunk; and the LaSalle Street Church was having a hoot, strangers to me after all.

I pinched my lips and watched the play unfold.

The woman came straight down to the front. She tucked her body sideways into the third pew on my right-hand side, never casting so much as a glance at me. She thumped to sitting and then proceeded to open the bag on her lap, to root therein all mindless of the place, the time, the worship, the people—and to place her worldly possessions on the seat beside her. She had a glittering eye, precisely like a weasel's.

Well. I raised an angry face to the congregation and only then discovered that they were as much the butt of this joke as I was. The poor usher, when he caught my eye, literally threw up his hands in apology. Some of the members sent me stricken looks, aggrieved that such a thing should happen in their church. Others raised eyebrows of incredulity. They didn't believe it either. They thought it must be a setup and that I myself had found a tricky way to make my Robert real to them.

Ah, Jesus—nobody's joke, then? A baglady indeed?

No, I wasn't angry anymore. I was plain scared, and all my wretched nerves returned. What was I supposed to do with a baglady here? The story of Robert was a story of my sin, was meant to say, *Don't sin as I did.* How could I continue to tell that story faithfully, effectively, and at the same time ignore this baglady—and so commit the sin again, again? Well, I would be lying in my teeth.

The story of Robert was meant to be a story. An illustration. Not an event. Jesus, please: I had come here to preach, not to be sifted like wheat in public. So what was I supposed to do?

But people all over the church, no longer smiling now, were looking at me, awaiting the next move. I had no other move than the one I'd planned.

Therefore, *I kept on preaching*, I said into the microphone, swallowing prodigious loads of spit, drawing a baleful smile across my face. *And Robert kept on rocking. When I preached quietly it didn't matter*, I said. *He kept rocking. When I preached louder, it mattered. He rocked the harder. And soon he began that threatful Baptist practice—clapping. I felt the trickle of sweat on my spine—*

Nobody laughed. Somebody should have laughed at the humor. That is, somebody would have laughed under other conditions. But Robert was here in the form of the baglady. You can't gossip about the person who is listening to you. Nobody laughed. The people were anxious, rather, discomfited by my talking, which could be slurring her. I was losing them, O Lord. They were repudiating me. Strangers.

Well, then I had no choice.

I had to acknowledge the baglady.

I stepped down out of the chancel, dragging the microphone wire behind me, and walked across the little distance that separated me from the mumbling lady. I approached the third pew, and spoke to the woman herself.

I raised my voice in spite of myself, I said into the microphone, directly to this woman. *And Robert began to stomp*, I said.

The woman narrowed her eyes and pierced me with weasel glances, as sharp as the needles of hair round her head. She hissed a sentence at me, a challenge, in fact. I heard the words but kept on preaching.

All at once, I said, *Robert threw his two arms in the air and roared, "I'm going to pray!" I stopped cold. Robert, too, was stunned—*

The baglady jumped backward and frowned in serious doubt for my sanity. She put her hand to her bosom, which was cased in several layers of shirt.

Robert, I said to the woman as gently as I could, but I boomed in the microphone, *Robert considered the wonderful promise he had produced, to pray, but I stood mute with panic, because his prayer was a threat to me. Do you understand that?*

I meant the question for the people. But the baglady compulsively shook her head.

I was afraid of his prayer, I said. *I didn't want to lose control of things. But things went from bad to worse. "Yessir!" Robert shouted, "I'm going to pray!" "Robert!" I cried, and I dived for him—*

In fact, I reached my left hand toward the woman as though she were my Robert. But even before I touched her shoulder, she trapped the hand and began to fumble for something on the pew.

"Robert, you can't pray," I cried. "Why not?" he said. And I said—

But at that moment in the LaSalle Street Church I said nothing at all. I was silenced, and my story stopped.

The baglady had found what she was feeling for. She snatched it up between us—almost like some talisman against an evil—and she hissed a second sentence with startling clarity, and my neck began to tingle. But what she held was a half-pint carton of milk. And what she was doing was giving it to me.

I heard an expulsion of air, a sigh from the congregation. I interpreted their sigh. The drama around me diminished me, and I was moved, and the microphone sagged away from my mouth.

Behold: the impoverished is nourishing the preacher. Behold: the servant is being served.

I remembered the microphone and lifted it again. My voice continued in an amplified squeak: *"You can't pray because we have a time to pray," I said, and the little man collapsed before me—*

But this woman with spikes of white hair and tiny weasel eyes was willful, insistent. She shook the carton of milk. She wanted me to take the milk. I did. I took the milk in my left hand, then she nodded once, fiercely, as though satisfied with my obedience, and dismissed me by folding her arms across her bosom.

•   •   •

Umbrella canes, twin peaks of a picked-out hair, collection plates, and a dollar bill as soft as a handkerchief—I brought my story to its conclusion. I made whatever points it occurred to me to make. And then I retreated to my chancel seat, which was hidden from the people by a massive pulpit.

Amen, amen, I was grateful to be hidden.

No, I wasn't nervous anymore. A bit overwhelmed, perhaps, that my story had been no story at all, but a holy assault, and that my sermon had been preempted by reality. "Angels in the form of the oppressed"—indeed. God was in this baglady. Whether the LaSalle Street Church was aware of that or not, I was.

And yet I could have explained the awe in me, if awe was all it was.

What I could not have explained—what might have looked like insolence, and why I was glad to be hidden— was that my mouth kept smearing into a grin and my chest kept pumping toward an outright laugh. I wanted to laugh. Every time I thought of what it was the baglady had actually said to me, I covered my mouth to keep from laughing.

Angels, yes indeed! But when angels descend from Cabrini Green and not from condominiums, they don't bathe first; they don't approve themselves with pieties first; they do not fit the figments of Christian imagination: they prophesy precisely as they are and expect us to honor them whole, prophecies and blasphemies together.

I wanted so badly to laugh, because God was roaring a wonderful thunder, surely. The baglady had been a joke, yes—and the joke was God's.

When I had first approached her pew, all crippled with fear, this is what the crook-backed woman hissed at me: "It's damn if I will," she said. "It's damn if I want to, Preacher. You'll never get me to stop my swearing!"

What would the La Salle Street Christians make of that? My ears uncorked to hear her. But I drove my story onward nonetheless.

And when she handed me the carton of milk, when all of the people exhaled their sentimental sigh, she sharpened her weasel-gaze and hissed: "This—is—poison. Hee-hee! Hee-hee!"

The messenger of God was cracked. And so was I, to her shrewd eye. Oh, we were a subversive pair in this rational middle mix, Americans at worship. They had no idea what sedition they'd taken to their bosoms—

And God was pounding his thighs and weeping with the laughter surely.

This is the end of the story of Robert.

I went back to his dim-lit room, and with no embarrassment asked to see his cardboard box again.

He saw nothing strange in my request. He pulled the box from underneath the sink, and he repeated his offer as though nothing at all had occurred between my first and second visits:

"Anything, Reverent," he said. "Anything you want."

I took my time deciding. Finally I selected a trivet with two legs. We agreed. It was an excellent, tasteful choice.

8

Hamilton

Paul was in the fifth grade. I was in the sixth. As we had in Chicago several years ago, so here: we walked to school and home again. There was only an open field between the house and the schoolyard, and Mother figured she could police our goings and comings from the kitchen window while she did the dishes.

A practical and obdurately ethical woman was our mother. She had fought many a brave fight on her children's behalf, and now the bravest of all was for our souls, that we be found righteous in the assizes. That is to say: she kept an eye on us.

If in church on a Sunday morning we could not behave (and she could not reach us), at home on a Sunday afternoon we enacted another sort of church, wordless, spare, and twice as long. The Church of a Perfect Discipline. We sat on a backless bench in sacred silence, our bodies enchained by the eyes of our mother (who could quickly reach us), that our hearts and our consciences might be free.

She had accepted grimmer challenges than ours in the past, and had prevailed: Jimmy Newman's grandmother (remember her?) had bitten a bitter dust; black bear in at least three national parks had woofed and retreated from the pans and spoons of our mother's clangorous ire; blizzards on the plains of North Dakota had not killed nor blenched a child of hers. And the murderous malice of gossip, the cold human enmity in Edmonton, Alberta, where we now were living, our mother outfaced with biblical immobility.

She made a fortress of the forms of our religion. She

guarded the doors of that fortress like Peter with a short sword and a key. And though this may seem small to the world at large, to us it was the fate of the children of martyrs—that Mother on a Sunday, when other worshipers were too ignorant to know the proper times for rising, rose, rose grandly, and commanded her children to rise up with her. So we alone would stand in the midst of a whole congregation, gazing staunchly forward, making our stance a lesson to them all, heaping coals of fire, as it were, upon their heads—but suffering the scorch in our own poor foreheads.

Ah, Mother was Amos in Bethel. Mother was Paul in Jerusalem. Mother was Christ in the courts of the Temple. Fearless. And practical. Obdurately ethical. Ours.

We would be found righteous.

Or perhaps we would be found like her for sheer independence and outrageous spunk.

In Alberta, Canada, in the latter part of November, the evenings come cold and early. In the year that Paul and I were in the fifth and sixth grades at Virginia Park School, the cold came dry and mean and snowless; the sky hung low and grey; the earth was bone-hard, frozen, dead.

It was dusk, then, when I hit the crashbars and burst through the door into the schoolyard. It was four o'clock in the afternoon, and I was racing because I was late. There were right and wrong times, right and wrong places to be—and at four o'clock, home was right; practicing the piano was righter; and school was the wrongest place of all to be.

I hadn't even zipped my parka. I had books in both hands. Running at top speed I could be home in less than five minutes.

But when I wheeled around the corner, I saw that the schoolyard wasn't empty yet. Fifteen boys, maybe twenty boys, remained in the dying light, all of them bunched in a circle and making an unholy noise, and in spite of myself my feet slowed down, and my interest was hooked, though none of the boys noticed me since all of them were huddled inward, and I stopped.

It was a fight, of course. A fight always took that shape in the schoolyard, a sort of wandering, swollen centipede, a knot of excited boys that shifted ground as the two fighters in the middle maneuvered to and fro.

Or it would be a fight as soon as one of the fighters threw a punch. As long as the circle was moving, the fighters weren't fighting. They were still circling one another, still threatening horrible things to come, still working their bloods up in talk and taunt, each calculating his reputation against the pain of an honest punch, each hoping the other would fold in fear and quit. As long as the boys who formed the ropes of the ring were screaming and still getting madder, it wasn't a fight yet.

I began to walk around the circle, rising on tiptoe, trying to get a view inside. It was cold out here. It would be hot in there. They probably had taken their parkas off, though they would be puffing clouds of steam.

All at once a silence stunned the air, and a gasp went up from the round animal, the boys in a bunch. Someone had thrown a punch. I wanted more badly to see. I put my books down and started toward the circle.

A head popped up and saw me coming. The mouth opened and formed my name, but I couldn't hear it because of a sudden, bloody roaring. The head belonged to a tall kid named Craig, who started immediately to swim through the mob in my direction.

When he broke free, he threw out his arms to stop me.

"Keep it clean," he yelled at me. "Keep it clean!"

What did he mean, *Keep it clean?* I never fought. I had worn glasses from the third grade on. Marcia Jespersen had told everyone that I walked like a girl, and as humiliating as the observation was, she was right. I was intimidated by your casual comments—forget about your boyhood brawls!

But this tall fork, this fool, this Craig who was freckled past any restraint of conscience, whose neck stuck out all bony like a buzzard's—he was absolutely serious. "Keep it clean!" he yelled at me, a genuine wariness in his eye. Why would I want to make it dirty? Unless—

Oh, my poor heart began to go pipping like the rabbit's, and my sight unfocused, and Craig just disappeared.

My brother was in the middle of this ring! That's why the fight was personal. And Craig's friend Hamilton was his adversary; that's why Craig would expose himself to keep me out. Paul was in the fifth grade, Hamilton was in the sixth. My ears and all my head began a buzzing. This was terrible. The world was terrible. What was I going to do if my brother was in a fight?

I thought just nothing in that moment, but walked mechanically toward the circle of boys. Craig danced at my shoulder. I didn't notice. I dropped my parka. Boys began to open a path for me. I scarcely saw their faces: I was suffering a simple dread, and my whole body was another thing. It didn't belong to me.

When the circle parted to the very center, when I saw Jamie Hamilton astride my brother, drawing his right fist back to hit Paul's innocent eyes, I lost all sense, and I exploded.

Jamie Hamilton, Jamie Hamilton, that rat of a greasy face! Hambones, we called him. Ham-'n-eggs, we jeered between ourselves, my brother and I. He called us "Christians," making bathroom sounds in his armpit: "Chrissssssstians!" He lisped the word and meant that we were fairies. He shamed us in public and forced us in private to doubt the value of a faith that caused such wretchedness, such vile disgrace. Jamie Hamilton—O dear Jesus, how we hated him! And he was going to hit my brother?

No, by God! I simply exploded. I ruptured into something new, Defender of Everything, of Faith and Paul and Truth—

I torpedoed Hamilton with the top of my skull, an inglorious launching of myself, and knocked him off my brother and scrambled to my feet before he did; and the instant I saw his pagan face arising from the ground, I cocked my arm and hit it: *Crack!*

There was a distinct, an almost dainty sensation in that *crack* that satisfied my knucklebone and filled me with an inexpressible pleasure. I'd broken his nose. And then it was breathtaking to me, how suddenly and beautifully the blood bloomed all around his mouth. He gurgled. He touched his lip. And then the eyes of Jamie Hamilton went wide with shock when he saw the blood that he brought away.

That fast, the fight was over.

I stood up with a wild sense of well-being. I hardly heard the bubbles of approval the other boys were popping as they made a way for Paul and me. The delayed rush of adrenaline was glory enough for me, true to the Truth till death. Mock me now, O Jamie Hamilton!

We strode home in a grey light, did not run, did not forget our books, did everything exactly right except, perhaps, the meeting of the deadline. We would be very late, of course; but I didn't think it would matter. Not on my shield, but carrying it, I came.

As it turned out, my mother didn't even mention the lateness of our arrival. Nor did she send me downstairs to practice piano. Nor did she so much as interrupt us, Paul and me, when we recounted in epic detail the battle won and done. We were giddy now, who had been noble on the field.

But if she chose to pass over our tardiness, it wasn't because for once the tardiness was right. Rather, she perceived a still more ominous sin in her son, a greater wrong which wanted immediate and exclusive attention.

"So?" I said when my story was finished, grinning, awaiting some reaction from my Lycurgus. Mother was gazing into a fry pan of potatoes, stirring with her right hand, her left hand on her hip. I couldn't read her expression. She had an even brow and a straight nose upon which I focused when she talked, because the talking always dipped the tip of it. From infancy I liked her nose. It is, in fact, the very first memory I have of her, the pelican's wing of sympathy, the eagle's wing of strength.

"So?" I said.

"You fought," she said.

I said, "I did."

"And you think it's finished," she said.

I said, "I do." More finished than ever before with Jamie Hamilton. The night was black outside the window now.

My mother said, "You're wrong."

Wrong. Obdurately, Mother was ethical. "Wrong" did not mean mistaken or inaccurate. "Wrong" was opposed to "right." It meant "unrighteous." It meant there was a sin abroad, and she had the right to right it.

This was not the direction I thought our conversation would take. I gazed at her profile, which was bright from the light on the stove, and said nothing. Her eyes were intent on potatoes.

"You hit Mr. Hamilton," she said.

"Hambones," I said compulsively. "Jamie," I said more properly. And then, more softly, I said, "Yes." That had been, before this spare interrogation, my triumph. Yes. I hit Hamilton.

"And he bled?" she said.

"Mom, I broke his nose! I told you that."

"Don't take a high tone with me, young man," she said. "You hit Mr. Hamilton. Did he bleed?"

"Yes."

"Wash your hands," she said. "Sit. Eat supper. You and Paul will give him time to compose himself."

All my joy began to drain away from me. I felt weak and weaker, even while I looked at the tip of my mother's nose.

A heavier duty than battle was emerging in the kitchen, a dead-load duty. The night outside was cold Canadian winter, and black.

"And then you will go to Mr. Hamilton," my mother said. "You will apologize for the injury you gave him—"

"He's a bully!" I cried out. "Mom, he's always mocking us!"

"He is. He does," she said. "What he does doesn't matter. What you do does."

"Oh, Mom! He doesn't deserve apologies. He deserves exactly what he got. Mother, please!"

"But you did not deserve to give it to him. You fought. You hit him. He bled. Period. You will apologize to Mr. Hamilton. This discussion is at an end."

And so were the potatoes, which she took steaming from the stove. And so was the glory I'd earned that afternoon by blunder and luck. And that was the point: it happened once by accident; it would never happen again. Surely I could have enjoyed my spasm of heroism a while before it vanished. Surely I shouldn't have to destroy it myself. What did she know of the troubles we had in school?

I ate no potatoes, none, that night.

Paul and I walked in parkas down Ada Boulevard, down the middle of the street, because there was no sidewalk there. Neither of us said a thing. There was an icy wind come cursing from the river. My face was stiff, my cheeks were numb, immobile from the cold.

These are the things I hated then. I hated mittens, as opposed to gloves, because your hands were rendered infantile, like penguin flippers. I hated the parka hood tied tight around your face, as opposed to a stocking cap, which everyone who had one called a tuque. I hated parkas generally because they bound your body in a bunting, the way we had to wear them, and made a baby of a boy eleven

years old. I hated that your lips chapped in the winter if
you licked them. I hated that it hadn't snowed. I hated Paul
for pie-faced innocence. I hated fried potatoes. I hated
school. I hated rules. I hated this, *this!*

The night sky was a wilderness, mute. The stars had no
responsibilities.

You could see the insistent flag of your breathing.

Paul blew steam to the moon. I hated that he wasn't hating
anything.

We walked round to the side of Hamilton's house, where
there was a yellow porch light shining. I rang the doorbell
with an impossibly mittened hand.

In a little while the inner door opened with a suck of air.
The storm door was opaque with frost. A darker figure on
the inside fiddled with the lock, and then it was Hamilton's
mother who peered out, clutching her collar at the throat.
She had a modern hairdo like Donna Reed. That shocked
me. She looked young.

"We hab to talk to Jamie," I said. I could hardly make my
mouth work on account of the cold; but my heart ran hot,
an ill-fitted pump leaking blood into my chest. I hated the
mumble my mouth made of my words. I hated the way I
was feeling right that instant: supplicating and scared at
once. But Mrs. Hamilton prolonged the distress by saying
nothing, merely glaring at me from a haughty profile. No,
she didn't look young. She looked put-together. Assembled.
Like she bought the pieces in a store.

"You're Wally," she said.

I nodded.

"You fractured James's nose today."

I nodded balefully.

Paul twittered, "Broke it," and I hated him for that.

"I hope you have the goodness to thank God for your
mother," said Mrs. Hamilton. "Come in."

We entered a warm landing, stairs to the basement in front

of us, three steps up to the kitchen on our right. I was dumbfounded at the cleanliness of the house, and the scent of ginger. I thought Hambones lived in filth.

His mother signaled us to stay put. She went in through the kitchen, and we stood with our arms stuck out, a ridiculous backward tilt to our spines as we watched her go. The parkas put a lock on our necks. I looked like a child. But I was ancient and lean and haggard with a wasting hatred. I hated. I simply, with all my hot heart, *hated*—and I wished to God that there was something truly worthy of the rage in me.

My glasses had fogged. I took them off and began to rub them between the thumb and the shapeless mitten-fingers.

Then Jamie Hamilton darkened the kitchen above us. I tipped my swaddled body back to squint at him. I say, In a parka in order to move your head you must arch your entire body. I say, This is the constraint of humiliation. I jammed my glasses on my face.

Hamilton had a neat bandage taped on the bridge of his nose. Too neat. That made me mad. I wished it were an explosion of cotton batting. But there were bright red scallops under either eye. Good. I had done that.

One of my glasses stems had bent to the outside of my parka hood. Unsettled lenses, they tilted my vision. I let it go.

Hamilton, with a thin face, free in his socks and pants and flannel shirt, said, "What," staring down on us.

Through a cold blubber of lip I declared, "Mby mbom says we got to say we're sorry." And I said, "We're sorry."

"What?" said smarmy Hamilton, smiling, delighted. "You're what?"

Now and forever I will remember that in spite of myself, spontaneously, I actually took a posture of repentance. It had been my mother's command, not my own desire, and therefore not truly my own words. Nevertheless, to say *sorry* caused sorrow to be written in my body, so trained was I in

the way that I should go. I bowed my head in apology; and
that, of course, bent my whole self down before the egre-
gious Hamilton. Servile. In a humble voice I repeated,
"Sorry." And my glasses clattered to the floor.

At once, I reached for them—and I uttered a dirty curse.

Even before I straightened again I heard a sound above
me, the hiss of a lisping sound. I squinted upward, tilting
backward. I saw that the face of Jamie Hamilton had twisted
itself into the ghastly mimic of a smile. And he was whispering, barely audibly, "Chrisssssssstian"—

Heavenly Father, hatred soared in me with a sort of jumping jubilation. And I liked it! Oh, I rejoiced in it. Because
all at once I'd found the righteous target of all my rage, the
thing that deserved my most violent detestations, a thing of
such sturdy repute as to stand my anger:

Christianity!

That is how I endured the humiliation of having bowed
to Hamilton, of having manifested any weakness in me. I
hated religion with an extravagant hatred. From that moment I conceived and cherished dire convictions against the
faith of our mothers, holy faith; and I grew a span in mine
own eyes; and I survived the sixth grade with my honor
intact.

9

Jolanda Jones

Joe and Selma Chapman—a retired couple, he with a homburg, she with a stole, he with his white shoes, she with the smile of a Rockwell Madonna, both with the presumptive airs of the successful and the childlike air that everyone knows that they're successful—had their own pew at Grace. Four from the front, on the right-hand side, facing Jesus. They sat by the wall.

They hadn't bought the pew, of course, nor paid some sort of pew fee, nor affixed (as have other traditions) plates with their names to the aisle-side crest of the pew. They just always sat there. It was just known, by any whose knowledge was worth a nickel. Perhaps they'd left their scent on the wood.

Nor were they unique at Grace. Many of the faithful honored ritual and tradition by making possession nearly an eleventh commandment—though no one ever spoke of it: *Thou shalt stick to thine own pew.* Or, since commandments generally take a negative turn: *Thou shalt not trespass on thy neighbor's pew.* There was a practicality in this, and a personal gratification as well, because you could come late to worship without fear of lacking a seat. Everyone had remembered you in your absence, had respected your position in the church, had preserved a place for you. *Come up, come up, dear Joe and Selma Chapman, gentlefolk honored among assemblies. See? We've saved your seat for you. Come, though we've begun the feast. Occupy the pew, which is your due.* Something like that. Even so do Christians, or members of Grace at least, relish the trappings of reputation together with a little modest praise.

And it were best unspoken; that's the Christian characteristic of this praise: its modesty, its pious restraint. Pew space does it nicely, doing it mutely. It is simply, silently *known*. And the less that has to be said about it, why, the deeper strikes its root into the community: "These," no one says unto another, because no one has to; everyone knows, "these are people of repute. Give place to them."

Or maybe Christians need the security of custom. Maybe it merely unnerves them to have to take a different perspective on the pastor Sunday after Sunday. Let sightings be as stable as the faith itself. Let worship be as changeless as God. The world is chancy enough. One room at least, and one community, should fit the Christian as familiarly as the hug of her mother, especially when that Christian has grown old and childlike again.

So Joe and Selma had their pew, though no one advertised as much.

And things went well—so long as everybody knew as much.

But what of the stranger, who would surely come to church in ignorance? Ignorance is a test of Christian virtue. Perhaps we should nail nameplates to the pew-wood after all.

Even ten minutes before the service was scheduled to begin, there sat in Joe and Selma's pew a woman of unconscionable beauty—and a kid of doubtful breeding. The kid had an animal gleam in his eye, and canine teeth, I'd bet, if he opened his mouth and grinned. But the woman had eyes that seized my attention and smoldered in my mind as I bustled about the chancel, preparing for worship.

Her eyes had a catlike slant, a natural black line embor-

dering the lid, a shining white and a steadfast penetration
as dark as charcoal, lashes as long as luxury. She gazed at
me with direct watchfulness. This was a bit disturbing, to be
so brazenly stared at by a stranger—as though some question had been asked and I had left it unanswered, but she
was waiting, but I didn't know what the question was. And
this was the more disturbing, because she was so beautiful;
I couldn't shut her out. Her cheekbones formed an aristo-
cratic V, and her mouth was fine, so fine, *re*fined. Nor could
I dismiss her gaze as admiration or curiosity. It was neither
of those. It had some particular meaning. Some appeal in
it.

So—perhaps five minutes to worship—I walked over to
the fourth pew and smiled and offered my hand, introduc-
ing myself as the pastor. The kid lit up like Christmas. He
grinned. He did not have canine incisors, but a row of tiny,
separated teeth and a giggle that hinted insanity. My presence, it seemed, electrified him, and he drummed his heels
on the pew, two years old. She never removed her eyes from
me nor tempered their intensity. But her mouth said that
her name was Jolanda Jones, that you spelled Jolanda with
a *J*, even though you pronounced it with a *Y*, and that "this
here's Smoke," meaning the kid, that his name was Smoke.
Her talk surprised me. It was neither beautiful nor aristo-
cratic. It was sheer street, the aggressive rhythms of Lincoln
Avenue. I stumbled on that difference between the dark
beauty of her eyes and the flat assault of her speech.

After a moment's hesitation I welcomed her and retreated—nothing resolved. I mean, her eyes still asked a
question I had not comprehended. And I had neglected to
mention that she could, if she wished, take another pew. Or
that we had a nursery where children might be more com-
fortable. Worship began with nothing resolved.

And if Jolanda Jones caused confusion in me, what do you
think she did to the other good people of Grace?

Folks stood up to sing the first hymn, directing their at-

tention to the front. But folks, when the hymn was done
and they sat down, quickly redirected their attention to one
who was slower at sitting, unused to the up-and-downing of
Lutheran ritual: to Jolanda Jones. And then their eyes
popped open and church got interesting, and I had a difficult time reminding folks that I was there, leading them in
confession of their sins.

Not only did Jolanda Jones possess an unreasonable
beauty, but she dressed it (so said their eyes) "like Satiday
night on Sunday mornin'!" No skirt, no blouse on her. A
dress. But even a pants suit would have been more sanctified
than such a dress: low in the back (and most of the folks
apprised her from the back), loose on the shoulders, utterly
missing below the knee, and as tight on the hips as taste on
a minister's tongue. She wore a hat. Well, grant her that—
she covered her head in church. But this hat swept left from
the side of her head and brushed one bare shoulder with a
black feather. Black. That hat was a midnight black. The
dress, it was resplendent black. And black were the long
Egyptian eyes she never removed from me. Devout were
some of the eyes on her, and pious were other eyes; but I
don't think it was the absolution which I was pronouncing
that caused devotion in certain men and piety in certain
women.

I do believe Jolanda Jones felt the force of the piety of
those eyes, because her fine mouth pinched. But she didn't
blink; and her head and her hat, she held them high. And
then—just as I rose to the lectern for the reading of the
Scripture lessons—Joe and Selma Chapman arrived at
church. If opinions regarding our visitor had been mixed
before this, they certainly began to harden now.

Selma came up the aisle first. Joe, her gallant, was hanging
his homburg in the narthex. He entered at the back of the
church, smiling and nodding, receiving quiet greetings from
the deacons and such friends as had their pews in the rear.
He shook a hand, he patted a shoulder. But when he was

halfway to his pew, he raised his eyes and saw a piteous sight: Selma *confounded*.

Poor Selma was literally circling in the aisle like a hopeless satellite, confused, as though the common world had been transfigured and she didn't know where to go. She looked at her pew and found it full. She turned and looked away, reorienting herself to the whole room proper. Then she turned back to her pew again, and behold: it still was full. People were in it. And what a people they were! A mad little boy was grinning straight at her, and an extraordinary woman was *not* looking at her at all.

Selma Chapman uttered an anxious bleat.

Joseph Chapman rushed to the side of his wife. And since no amount of staring could shame Jolanda from the pew, he led poor Selma to seats much closer to the front, patting her shoulder, comforting her, and contemplating this wonder, that the Earth had tilted on a Sunday morning.

Well, and if the Earth had tilted, then it was not unlikely that storms should follow, a shaking of the elements.

When next I stepped into the aisle to preach, mad little Smoke sat bolt upright, excited by the sudden freedoms my freedom offered his own little self.

It was severely noted by folks in the congregation that this woman, whoever she was, put no restraints upon her child—indeed, paid him no mind throughout the entire time that others were trying to worship God. The kid lacked discipline!

Smoke stood up on the pew while I preached. He grinned at me; then all at once he squatted and flung himself into the air. That child sailed into the aisle, landed belly-flop and loudly, then proceeded to swim a sort of breaststroke up the floor in my direction. Giggling insanely at himself. So we had three noises in the church: my preaching, Smoke's fun, and the hennish sound of clucking in the pews.

But Jolanda Jones did not remove her gaze from me. It

grew sharper, more intense, increasingly an act of pure, dark will, a burning as beautiful and stinging as a scimitar.

And when the service had run its course and God had received what praise God could under the circumstances; when folks had arisen and filed out of the church (none speaking a criticism to the woman, such restraint also being characteristic of Christian piety); when that woman herself had finally, the last of all, come down the narthex steps with Smoke at her heels, I learned the question of her deep Egyptian eye.

Douglas Lander had been chatting the idle minutes with me. He caused a pleasant sense of ordinary peace whenever he talked, and for the moment I could almost believe that this was a Sunday like any other. Silver stems to the glasses on his filbert face, a mild and mobile smile, the little man had just begun to tell me the story of a childhood friend named William Quinn. Then Jolanda Jones—like the night of cloudless climes—darkened the steps above us, and Douglas's eyebrows twitched upward in a sort of glee.

"One o' them things," he murmured, and he disappeared, leaving the business to me.

"Good morning," I said. "Thank you for visiting—"

I don't think the woman even saw my hand extended. She prized me with her eye and straightway blurted her question:

"Is there a place for me in this church?"

Well, bless my soul! Well—of course. I assured her that of course there was.

She gazed at me.

I scrambled my answer in two directions. That is, I talked about the wideness of God's mercy, that it embraced everyone, everyone; and "God is in this place," I said. At the same time I gave her a brief description of the steps that anyone could take to join the congregation—urging her (as I did everyone) to go slowly over such an important decision.

Come back, of course. She ought to come back often in order to learn what sort of community she might be joining,
and whether it was compatible, and whether she believed as
we did, and so on, and so forth—

Through it all she gazed at me. When I ran out of words,
she said, "Is there a place for me 'n' Smoke in this here
church?"

I said, "Yes."

I meant it.

But she did not wholly believe me.

Jolanda Jones did come back again. Not immediately. In
fact, there was a longish period when we didn't see her at
all; and then, when she did return, it wasn't our welcome
but a particular urgency in her own life which persuaded
her to come. But she came. And she had made changes
which proved that the woman had not been unconscious of
the feelings of the people of the church. (How courageous,
I thought, to come full knowing! How deep her need must
be!)

Changes: she dressed, as it were, down to Christian tastes,
down to her shins and up to her neck. No hat. And she sat
in the very back pew on the right-hand side facing Jesus
(the pew the youth took for themselves). And she wore enormous sunglasses, covering a third of her face.

Those glasses declared her presence, to me at least, the
instant I turned to face the congregation and the service
began—her presence and her difference, both. Jolanda
Jones was trying hard to accomplish that whereof she had
no previous experience: to hide like a Christian among the
Christians. Never mind the heart. Her style was street-slick.
Her idiom betrayed her. She was working with a limited language, not learned in any Sunday School. Sunglasses on a
Sunday morning, indeed. And the regal nobility of neck and
cheekbone, the beauty that ached in the back of the room,

displaced her for sure. Those cheekbones hallowed her face like the wings of the seraphim. So if her style demeaned her, making her less than the normal Christian, her natural splendor exalted her above anything Christians could in good conscience call normal and therefore good. Either way the lady lost.

Changes, I said. She had pulled her black hair back in the bun of a Puritan. My heart went out to her.

But other things had not changed. Lo, the maniacal Smoke, her son! He could, it seemed, discharge himself from one pew as well as another. Down the aisle that gleeful child came swimming on his belly while I preached. Goodwill he offered to every grim Christian that sat on either side of him. Noise, noise the baby made, unaffected by judgments he did not feel. What *did* he feel? He felt himself to be a wonderful show. Obviously the kid lacked training, and his mother had no rods at home. And what did the Christians feel? Impotence. Helplessness in the face of such a rising up to play. Or else, by their expressions, constipation.

And this thing too remained unchanged, the question the woman had for me: *Is there a place for me? Is there room for someone like me in your church?*

"Good morning, Jolanda Jones," I said. I was shaking her slender hand. We stood in the tiny narthex. She had waited this time too until she was the last to leave the sanctuary, sitting as silent as midnight behind her blackened glasses, facing forward—and except for a little Smoke, we were alone.

She tipped her head to the side. The angle suggested she was looking at me, contemplating me. The glasses hid her gaze.

She said, "You 'called my name."

"Spelled with a *J*," I said. "But said with a *Y*. Right?"

A longer look this time. Smoke was pulling on my cincture as though it were a bell cord. I reached down and scratched behind his ears. The woman watched me do this.

Suddenly, "I wanna show you somethin'," she said, and she took off the glasses, gazing at me.

"Oh! I'm sorry," I said. And I was.

The right corner of her brow was angry with swelling. Blood vessels had ruptured in her eyeball, which was a hot, crimson red.

"Jolanda? You hurt yourself?"

"No," she said. "It ain't because I hurt myself." Her language banged against her beauty. But it fit her injury. "I didn't earn it neither," she said. "It was give me."

My voice grew tentative and low. All at once we were entering private territory. "Someone," I said, "hit you?"

"Hit me? Beat me!" she said, almost belligerently.

But her level eyes were asking, *Is there a place for me—?*

I felt an impulse to touch the wound, like a parent taking a child back home. It made her seem so vulnerable. But her tone was metallic, and her beauty too high for me. Her beauty would make my gesture something else. It stopped me.

"Did you see a doctor?" I said.

"Wouldn't do no good," she said, steady-eyed. "As far as this punch, it heals."

"*This* punch, Jolanda?" She was leading me by careful steps into her life. She was choosing each step as we went. The woman was not a fool. "There are other punches then?" I said.

"They been before," she said. "Why not again?"

Is there a place—?

"Jolanda," I said. "Forgive me for asking: who does this to you?"

"Smoke, behave," she said without looking at the child, probing, probing me with her long Egyptian eyes. "Smoke's bad," she said. And then: "My boyfriend."

"Your—?" Perhaps the woman was seeking some encouragement from me, a push from the preacher in obvious directions. Well, then the matter did not seem insoluble. "Just don't go out with him anymore," I said.

"Go out with him? Out with him?" she said. "*In* with him's more like it, Reverend." She paused. "We live together."

"Oh."

Jolanda was probing my face for every twitch, was weighing me in the balance: *Is there a place for someone like me in your church?*

"Your boyfriend," I said. "Beats you—at home."

"When he gets mad at me."

"Can't you—just leave him?"

"Why?"

For heaven's sake! Because he hurts you. Or maybe she was asking how much religion I intended to lay on her situation. I truly didn't know her meaning, because I didn't know Jolanda. And Smoke had hidden himself beneath my alb. And his mother had incredible strengths, the brazen ability to stare me in the eye without a blink of embarrassment. I was fumbling.

"Leave him," I said, "because he hits you. Isn't that the simplest solution?" If you're asking for solutions, that is. Are you?

"Then how'm I s'posed to feed Smoke?" said Jolanda Jones. "Smoke ain't his baby—"

I'm telling you me, Reverend. The me that's real. Is there room for someone like me—?

"—and it ain't too many men be willin' to put up with Smoke. He do. He give us a place, and we eat. And besides— we live together," she said as though that explained an enormous thing to me. She closed her mouth with a snap, and it looked so self-possessed, so hard, so elegant again.

What do you say to that, Reverend?

"But you showed me the bruise, Jolanda," I whispered. "But you hid it from the other people. Why did you show it to me?"

At first she gave her shoulders the slightest shrug, as though to say, Why not? Street, street: the flip Jolanda Jones.

But then she said, "Somebody—" and her voice caught, and her face grew tight with appeal. She surrendered a tiny gasp. She was suddenly terribly young, and the rest of her words came out in the sad humidity of need: "Somebody oughta know," she said. And for the first time, she dropped her eyes.

"Well," I said, a little breathless: so much she revealed to me; so moved was I by the intimacy and this sudden softness, the dropping of her eyes; at the same time, so stupid, so helpless! "Well, now I know," I said. "But what can I do for you?"

Immediately the street asserted itself. She popped the dark glasses back on, grew erect, and said, "C'me on, Smoke. We gotta go."

"Jolanda," I said, suddenly hasty, "you know that Jesus loves you, don't you?"

"Hey!" she said with a smirk. "Hey, what? Me *and* poor Smoke?"

"Of course, you and Smoke. Of course. This is Jesus."

"So, then." It was her mouth alone. Her eyes were concealed. "Me and Smoke can come to your church."

"Absolutely."

"And ain' nobody here goin' be tarred by that?"

"No."

"Smoke, he's bad. Smoke, he don' bother the people here?"

"No. Well—no. Well, I'll tell you what, Jolanda. Did you know there's a nursery where little kids might feel more at home?"

"C'me on, Smoke. We gotta go."

And she was gone.

Two times. Maybe three times Jolanda Jones appeared in

church after that. But the times were widely spaced, and now she left before the worship was over, so we didn't talk. Once Smoke was with her. Other times he was notably, as they say, absent—and I will admit my relief when I saw the mother without the son. Though I liked Smoke, that thick-necked, grinning libertine, that troubler of Israel.

The fact that we had a nursery began to appear in capital letters in the Sunday bulletin. But the fact that people had pews reserved for themselves, and the fact that they were discountenanced when others sat in their pews, were harder facts to publish. Folks started to come early to church. Jolanda had worked a wonder.

For myself, I thought of her sometimes while I sat in my study. I imagined the scenes I'd never seen, the abuse she must be suffering—and the flat sass with which she was capable of meeting that abuse. Even Egyptian Isis could be shrill, could scrap and scream a fury from the street. But I imagined as well the pain that she hid beneath her marvelous hardness, and I grew sorry all over again and miserable for her. What did she mean, "And besides—we live together"? How is living together, all by itself, a hold to *keep* them living together? Jolanda Jones had remarkable strengths. I had experienced them. Then why couldn't she just walk away from an abusive man? I mulled these things in my study late at night, my books forgotten. I didn't understand them. Or her: that godly comeliness, that grit, that yearning need.

Is there a place for me in your church?

Months after he began it, Douglas Lander finished his story about William Quinn.

He and I were standing on a corner of the church property, he with a rake in his hand, I with a small Communion set. I had been feeding the shut-ins bread and wine. He had been mowing the lawn. He pointed toward Governor Street.

"Used to live there when I was comin' up," he said. "Mm-mm. Mm-mm, that's goin' on a long, long time ago." The rake handle touched his jaw. "Had a sister. Had a brother. Had three beds in the bedroom. Had a friend."

"Douglas. A man like you, you had just one friend?"

He chuckled. "No," he said. "A friend in the bedroom. It was my mama could cook like a Martha, you know. Oh, she was magic at the stove. And she was liberal. Any somebody under our roof, that body could sit with us and eat. That's where I got my notions for giving food away, you know. From Mama. That's how we lived through the Depression, Lil an' me—never mind we had a flock o' children to feed. When we had the food, we give it away. When our friends had food, we ate. I lay that to Mama. I used to do some waiting in the dining car 'twixt here and St. Louis in the thirties. Ol' Bill Jones, he let me have the extra food, an' I took it home, and we give it away, yessir, yessir—"

Doug Lander leaned on the rake, remembering. This is how he used to talk, a meandering, peaceable journey through a not outrageous world. His memories were always consolations. His sing-song voice disposed me to patience.

"What was I saying?" he said. "Aw yeah. Mama's cooking. Well, William Quinn, he played at my house most the time when we were boys. He only lived—let me see. There. Just over there. But seemed he liked to come to my house after school. So then, he was there when we ate supper. An' Mama said, 'Sit, William Quinn,' an' he did. Eventually he was there for most our suppers. I said, 'William! Look like you live with us.' He got—I remember this—he got a peculiar look on his face, an' he said, 'Why not?' "

Douglas Lander dropped his head and began to laugh. He raked a stroke, laughing. I smiled with him.

"He had a good mama, 's I recall," said Doug. "Wasn't no nastiness in his house. But we walked on over to his house, an' he told his family he wanted to live with us, and no one said no. So he got a pair of pajamas an' his baseball. Three beds in my bedroom. One for me, one for my brother, and from that day on, one for William Quinn. We grew up to-gether. He was a good boy. Mama said she was goin' to grad-uation as much for William as for me. But I lay it to Mama's cookin', you see. You feed someone, you make him to home. Just one o' them things. . . . Pastor?"

"What?"

"You goin' to answer that?"

"What?"

Douglas chuckled. "I s'pose somebody's got to get the mule's attention first. The telephone's ringin' in your office."

"Oh!" I dashed for the fire escape and my door.

"Reverend?"

"Yes?"

"This the Reverend of the church?"

"Yes."

"Well, I gotta talk to you."

"Okay."

"No, I mean I gotta *talk* to you. What I mean, I gotta come *over* and talk to you."

"Jolanda Jones?"

"It's a problem, see? I need help on a problem. All right? So—can I come?"

"Of course. What—?"

"I mean right now. So. Can I come?"

"Yes, yes, Jolanda, truly. Come. I'll wait for you."

She hung up. There had been the sound of typewriters behind her voice, a mechanical clatter that didn't appreciate the panic in that voice. Wherever she was, she was alone—or so it seemed to me. Lost in systems that felt like forests full of a tangled undergrowth.

She rushed into my office. Douglas, behind her, smiled and closed the door.

"Downtown," she explained. "I walked. Broke m' damn heel. Oh, Lord!"

Suddenly the world was not peaceable. Jolanda's face had lost Egyptian repose. She was trembling when she sat, and she wrung her hands between her knees. I felt in myself her terror. It was genuine fright—but I didn't know why we were afraid together. I'd have to learn the reason piecemeal.

"Jolanda? What's the matter?"

"I ain't no good," she burst out immediately, "and what's going to happen for it is, he's going to beat me. Lord, he's going to beat me next to death, and what can I say? He's right. There's the beginning and the end of it. He's right!"

"Jolanda, who's going to beat you?"

"Him. My boyfriend."

"Why?"

"Because I deserve it."

"Why?"

"And what's gonna happen to Smoke, O Lord? Smoke's got nothing to do with this. He never had. He just is. He's Smoke."

"Jolanda! Why is your boyfriend going to beat you?"

Her eyes flew to mine, now, for the first time. They fixed on me, as though suddenly realizing that I was there. And then she began to shake her head left and right, and the fear that had sharpened her face turned into utter misery, and the poor face melted. "Jesus, Jesus, Jesus," she murmured, "I made such a mess of things, of everything. O Jesus, *I* am the mess—" but she was looking at me "—an' you can do to me what you want, but what about Smoke? It ain't none of it Smoke's own fault."

"Jolanda, talk to me."

"Is there a place for a baby in this church? Won't nobody laugh at Smoke, will they?"

"Jolanda Jones, there is room for both of you, for Smoke and his mother and both of you, yes! But you've got to tell me what's the matter. What happened to you?"

"No," she said, taking a deep, shuddering breath. "Not *to* me. What was done, I done myself. Reverend, I been to the clinic. I had a test. I think I got the VD." Her eyes on mine. The blazing, beautiful eyes beseeching me, and I struggled not to flinch, to give her a calm gaze of my own, untroubled—though I felt full of her trouble in my breast. She was wringing her hands.

"Well, if you do," I said, "they'll diagnose it. And they can cure it too, with penicillin."

"I know, I know," she said. "That ain't it. They made me tell them who I been sleepin' with the last six months. Reverend, I told them, don't you see?"

"Good." I didn't flinch. For her, sleeping around was not at issue. Well, then, Jesus: let it not be an issue for me. There was room—

"*Not* good!" she said. Her poor face twisted at the difficulties between us: how could she make me understand? "*Not* good. My boyfriend ain't had no one but me in all six months, don't you see? He been faithful to me. Me, I been passionate, and I been mad at him, so I went out on him. So I give the clinic the names of all the men. But I give them his name too, you see? Do you see? Reverend, do you see?"

I nodded because I ached for her. Her terror came in black waves over me. But I also shook my head because I didn't see, and I was so sorry for being such a fool.

"They gone *call* the names," she pleaded with me. "All o' the names. His name too. They gone say, 'Come in for a test, 'cause you might have the VD.' They goin' to say, 'Someone you been sleeping with has got it; you got it from her.' When my boyfriend hears that, who do you think that *her* can be? No one but me!"

Jolanda Jones began to cry, her eyes wide open, still beseeching me for something, something, understanding and—something. The tears tripped over her lids and streamed down her face.

But I had absolutely nothing for her, nothing to say. The world she lived in was outrageously complicated, dangerous.

"Reverend," she whispered, "he's goin' to know I got the VD. He's goin' to know I didn't get it from him. He's goin' to know that I been messin' round with other men. He's goin' to kill me. Oh, Jesus, he's goin' to kill me. And—" She paused. She closed her mouth upon this final misery and lowered her eyes and grew terribly still. "An' he's goin' to be right."

There. That was it. That was all of it.

And I had no answer. Silence filled my little study, and blame came down on me. What solutions did I know that she didn't? None. Or what theologies of Western Christianity could speak a comfort to Jolanda Jones in this particular calamity?

Should I tell her she brought it on herself? You pay the piper? The soul that sinneth, it shall—? She had already said that. So what should I say? Call the police?

Oh, Christian! Go and ask the Street about the police. See what sort of force they are for the Joneses. Good or bad, right or wrong, the Street will only use the Man as it has been used by the Man. Contemptibly. She'd never call the police. She had come to me—Jolanda, Jolanda!

Or what should I say? Leave him? I had said that and had run against a block I could not understand.

What could I say? Saying anything just now would be the same as saying nothing, no matter how right or true or good or godly the words I chose. Jolanda Jones was crying. Words were useless. And I, while I sat across from her, was almost crying too. My skin burned with sorrow for her. No, I was no authority. No, I did not feel like a Reverend. Just sorry. Sorry.

I stood up. I closed the space between us. I took her hand. She gave it to me and stood as well. And then I hugged her, and her bones were small, and there wasn't a scrap of sass, not a piece of street inside this woman. She pressed her face into my chest, and she wept. I stroked her shoulder. We were children together.

Jolanda. I am so sorry.

On the following Sunday I hugged her two times more. The second hug lasted several minutes, and the Chapmans, Joe and Selma, ran out of conversation between themselves, so long did they have to wait to shake my hand. They were reduced to a discourteous, hang-faced gawking.

The first hug was Jolanda's too, but only by indirection. In fact, I hugged her son.

For Smoke on that particular Sunday had come to church with his mother. But Smoke knew nothing of calamities. No, Smoke was as cheerful and unperplexed as ever. That buster launched himself, as ever, headlong into the aisle and swam his giggling breaststroke forward while I preached.

When he got to my feet, he began to yank my cincture. He pulled on the hem of my alb. That was okay. I bent down and gathered the scandal in my arms and rose up and continued to preach. For just an instant Smoke was impressed by the view from my height. He gazed at the valley of faces, while faces gazed doubtfully back at Smoke.

But then he started to grin at my cheek, so close to his. And then he made a cork of his thumb and plugged my nose. And then he began to root through my alb, squealing, "Candy? Candy?"

Preaching became a mite more difficult.

I had no candy for Smoke. But (it dawned on me in a celestial rush of knowledge) I did have food.

Smoke and me, we stepped up into the chancel while I continued to preach. We approached the altar of God. We lifted the lid of a silver ciborium and found therein a secret store of wafers of the thinnest quality. Smoke was entranced. I hefted him into the crook of my left arm, and one by one

I fed the child the wafers, the Communion host, the only bread I had to hand.

Once, just once, my hungry Smoke said "Crackers" in my ear, and he kissed me for that, and he settled down to a silent, contented munching.

Preaching came easily then.

And who was to blame my raid on the breadbox if it solaced a child and relieved a whole congregation therewithal?

When we hugged in the narthex, Jolanda said, "You don't hate Smoke, then, do you?" and she clung to me a long, long time. Jolanda herself had begun that hug. She made it last a season and a Sunday and a lifetime.

I said, "I don't hate Smoke. I love the fool."

"He ain' bad. He just a puppy," she said. "He'll hush for the hand that feeds him somethin'."

"No, he's not bad," I said. "And neither are you. And I'm getting smarter myself." Egyptian eyes. The tawny skin of the Cheops. A raven hair, a human soul, an embrace of the lightest bones, and an invitation home: "Jesus loves you, Jolanda Jones. Do you know that now? God loves the whole, bewildered, dreary lot of us," I said. "How else would I know that Smoke is a puppy? Feed the fool, you do make him to home. A smart man taught me that," I said.

Mr. Joseph Chapman coughed. His homburg perched tippily on the very top of his balding head. He coughed again. Selma Chapman got his hint before I did. So then the two of them produced a series of declarative coughings together. Smoke perked up and watched them a moment, then cried at the top of his lungs, "Rowf! Rowf!"

The boy had an aptitude for parody.

Three weeks later I heard a terrific banging on my office door—a kicking, it turned out to be. Nothing feminine about this summons. Something horsey, aggressive, imperious. I expected an angry neighbor or—I didn't know what. Not a woman. Certainly not the regal Jolanda Jones, in the slant of whose eyes met all that's best of dark and bright—

But there she was, and she was beaming a refulgent joy. It fairly took my breath away.

"I did it, Reverend!" she declared. "I did *do* it!"

In one arm she held Smoke, wild-eyed and feral as ever, himself exploding with her happiness. He laughed with his tongue between his teeth, spraying me.

In the other arm she cradled a portable television set.

"No VD, no phone calls to nobody—an' I left him!" she cried. "Hey, I left that sucker flat when he wasn't home to see. Took Smoke. An' I took my own TV!"

Ah, this was news. I myself began to grin.

"So, what I want to know is," Jolanda grew serious suddenly, almost devout: "could my own church use a TV set?"

10

Horstman

1.

I went to the infirmary twice that year.

The second time was for the closing of a three-inch, self-inflicted laceration of the right forearm. There was no doubt, that second time, why I was there. No doubt, no hesitation, little talk, much action. Blood and worry make a certain breed of people lean, and the nurse belied her size with a quick precision and a dash that surprised me. Part of me admired her sudden command, white sanity, and skill. She'd seemed rather a garrulous woman to me the first time I was under her care, grandmotherly and voluminous. But when she saw the red-soaked rag around my arm, and when she unwrapped it and we watched a fresh emergence of blood from the cave in my flesh, why, she grew lean and deft and quiet, and part of me admired her. The other part was bleeding merely and consumed with shame.

But regarding the first time I went to the infirmary: the cause was less clear then.

I was sick, that's sure. But whether in mind or heart or body first, I didn't know.

I needed a respite. I needed, truly, some sort of hibernation from the horrors of a boarding school I did not love and which did not love me—and something broke down in me, and I didn't argue, and I didn't try to be brave. I simply accepted the week away from everything, from classes, the dorm, the refectory, the gym, the chapel, the harrier faces of the other boys, and I slept.

It is certainly possible that my mind was as troubled as my body. I went to the nurse with a valid fever and spunk water in my veins; and yet, as silly as this sounds, I harbored the notion that the root cause of my breakdown was, in fact, a neon sign—a huge red neon advertisement shaped like a star and stuck in the night sky on the north side of the Twenty-Seventh Street viaduct. The Red Star Yeast sign.

I hated that sign. It was never just still. It was devised of a series of concentric stars which lit up in sequence, so that a single star seemed always to be expanding, always contracting, like a gorge, a bolus in the universe, a red mouth trying to vomit. In the center of the star was a clock, likewise lit in red: time made visible, time made loathsome to me, time in a deadbeat regularity, expanding and contracting with an impassive, purposeless power. No boy could argue with such a sign, with lurid time, because it did not acknowledge boys. It just was. When we drove across the Twenty-Seventh Street viaduct, I always saw it ahead of us on the left-hand side, and I couldn't help but watch it swelling, though it oppressed me. This is what made me sick.

Actually (I know this now), I loathed that sign because it heralded my boarding school.

My family was living in Chicago again; but I was attending a prep school for the Lutheran ministry, Concordia, in Milwaukee; I was a stripling adolescent. We would spend perhaps two hours on the road, my parents and I, driving me back to school after a holiday home. We would breach Milwaukee in the evening, cold city lights and houses and taverns—and even yet there might be twenty minutes' solace before Concordia. But when I saw that star I knew the trip was nearly over, and I despaired. I couldn't pretend anymore that we were going somewhere else. The Red Star Yeast sign was the abandonment of hope.

Reality:

In a very few blocks we would be parking at the dormitory, and my father would help me carry luggage to my room on the third floor while my mother waited in the car; and I would be forced to wear a face of tough camaraderie, to pose as though I liked the banter the boys would fling at me, because my father would be grinning, thinking he understood the feckless ways of boys, but I knew better—I knew the spite and the personal scorn behind that banter, and I hated the impostures I was driven to, and I suffered my father's respect for me because I was a fraud, and I feared deeply, deeply the alienation I would feel the moment my parents drove away: the open contempt of my classmates, the loneliness which was my only refuge from contempt, and the black mood, the melancholia, the heart's paralysis—homesickness. My mother would wait in the car: proud of me? Proud of me? And I would return to her with my father. And we would exchange the farewells that nearly killed me, but we would keep them adult, perfunctory; and she would expend her feelings on irrelevant advice, sounding somewhat angry because advice was her cover for emotion. Proud of me? Sick for leaving me. And then they would drive away. And by the time they were crossing the Twenty-Seventh Street viaduct south toward Chicago, I would be in my room, sitting at my desk, the black mood descending, an utterly wretched child staring at a wall upon which I had hung no pictures, shutting my ears to my roommates, determined, despite the monstrous days to come, not to cry.

So. That's the drill. It happened again and again with minor variations. When I was at home for a holiday, I could actually revise reality and invent some legend for myself, some Camelot. I could make my brother think that I was important, my parents think that I was happy—the standard-bearer for the Wangerins on fields of honor (where my father once had gathered glory, and his father before him). But when I saw the Red Star Yeast sign swelling in the black Milwaukee skies, I failed. Illusion fled me. Fact destroyed me: no, I was not worthy at all, but a squalid boy in grievous circumstance, a byword. I despised that sign, that symbol, that clock, that Bumble, that bloody red specter of a boys' school.

There was a horrid hierarchy of power at Concordia, at the bottom of which—

Actually there were two systems of power at Concordia, one official, the other unofficial, unacknowledged, covert, and cruel. Both were alike in being unrelievedly male. Men and boys in loud community together tend less to mercy than to law; and if the law officially is the imposition of reasonable restraints upon disorder, unofficially it is merely brutal.

OFFICIALLY: Each floor in Wunder dormitory—which housed the freshman and sophomore classes—was governed by two proctors, upperclassmen who had the authority to police and to discipline according to campus rules. (The school was hoary with traditions from the German *Gymnasium*. There is much that could be described about its ranks and subordinations of power, order, and authority, the methods and the language for administration of the same. I could write of its curriculum: Latin, German, Greek, theology. I could write of chapel and the inscriptions on the walls above our heads: *Ora et labora, Ad maioram gloriam Dei, Sola fides*, and so on. I could write of the symbolic seating and the customs that prevailed in the refectory, where boys had and knew their places. But none of that is necessary here. One line alone is enough to draw a picture that otherwise repeats itself.)

In the hierarchy above them, the proctors reported to the dean, a square-jawed man with a rumpled face, a gravel voice, ice-blue eyes, and a legendary reputation, Zeus of the thunderbolts. Below them, the proctors had us. They checked to see that the dorm was cleared for chapel, morning and evening. Attendance was compulsory. They examined the cleanliness of our rooms weekly, and daily the meticulous making of our beds. They satisfied themselves, during evening study hours—also compulsory—that we indeed were studying. They could do this without entering our rooms, because each door had a window through which they peered while standing in the hallway. At ten thirty, lights were extinguished and boys were in bed—and again, the proctors used that window for patrolling. I always had difficulty falling asleep. I gazed at that rectangle of light. I saw the silhouette of the proctor hover there and then pass on. I heard the whip-crack of his heels on the cold stone floor. I heard his walking the hallway of Wunder dormitory. I tried to pray.

The proctors had, too, a certain discretion in creating new rules when they saw the need.

Early in the year one of my roommates sat batting a tennis ball against the wall with his racquet, an innocent pastime, I would have assumed. But the proctor appeared and on the spot laid down a law with such force I was astonished. "*Strafarbeit,* Reinking!" he cried.

Perhaps he'd had a bad day. Perhaps he'd had too much of tennis balls and indoor volleying. Even now it seems an outsized punishment—but then it chilled me with wonder: how powerful these proctors were, how stern their measures, and how terribly careful I must be regarding the rules! I sat at my desk, staring, afraid.

"No sports in the dorm, you got that, Reinking?" demanded the proctor, a fellow with a horsey nose which he thrust forward in his anger. "No knocking tennis balls about! No tennis in your rooms! None! That goes for all of you." His gaze included me. "And you, Reinking—you got two hours *Strafarbeit* tomorrow after classes. See me then." *Strafarbeit:* punishment work. The proctor departed.

Reinking's face was red, though his posture swaggered. "What are you lookin' at?" he snapped at me.

"Nothing," I said, dropping my eyes.

"No, nothin'," he mimicked. "You never mess up, do you?

You sit at your desk like Matilda. You girl!" My roommates could make that word sound vulgar, a contemptuous length of burp: *Girl!* Reinking said, "You're not so perfect. You'll screw up. You'll get caught with your panties down, swinging racquets the same as me—see if you don't."

"I won't," I said.

"Oh, kiss off, Wangerin." Reinking dismissed me with a gesture. "Kiss off!" he said.

But my righteousness was the one thing I clung to for salvation. I said "I won't" with serious conviction. Not only did I fear the consequences of "screwing up," the disgrace and the punishment, but I also preserved my self-respect and my identity that way—in my own mind at least. I was good, please. I was good. I was innocent and good. The obedience my mother had schooled me in was the one acceptable characteristic that set me apart from the others. It explained with some honor the suffering I endured in this place: Wangerin in the world, yes, he was different. He was good! No, Reinking, I would not screw up. I would maintain my righteousness, even to the heavens.

UNOFFICIALLY: Bigness and age gave power and advantage to certain boys, to upperclassmen generally. Smallness and childishness had few rights and no defenses. Tears were execrable. Cowardice, damnable. Fear excited the blood of your betters.

Therefore keep a passive face when seniors beat the bones of your shoulders with knuckled fists. This was their privilege. Someone had done it unto them.

"Wangerin! Hey, Wangerin!"

"What?"

"Wanna play a game with us?"

"What game?"

"Tell us which one hits the harder."

So: *Bang!* on the left shoulder. *Bang!* on the right.

"Okay, Wangerin. Who wins? Who's got a swing he can be proud of?"

A tentative pointing: "Him?"

"Hell, what about me?"

"Well—"

"Rematch! Rematch!"

Bang! on the right shoulder. *Bang!* on the left.

And so forth.

But keep a passive face. The best you can do is file it for the future, when your turn will come and you've earned the right of creative cruelty—

But I thought I would never exercise that right, if ever I got so far. I would remember my hurt and my humiliation; the chain of pain would stop with me, in me. Thus the difference between me and these: I would maintain my righteousness to the heavens. I would never bruise the spirit of another human. But these! Even these, the younger students at Concordia, my classmates: were pitiless. I saw them on an autumn afternoon annihilate a man.

Albert Burns was a mild professor of Old Testament who had never learned the expedience of a passive face. Though he was faculty, his status did not protect him because his mildness was read as meekness, and meekness dropped him to the bottom of the unofficial power structure. My classmates held him in contempt. Was he also contemptible? No, not by nature. He was balding; his arms were thick with a gentle hair; his voice was mild; *he* was mild. But this is the treacherous, frightening fact which I learned that day: that contempt can make a man indeed contemptible. The action calls forth its own validation. Yes, in the end he was a sadly contemptible figure.

"Burns beats his wife."

While Albert Burns was writing on the chalkboard, his back to the class, George Fairchild lowered his mouth into his hands and began a low and rhythmic murmur, barely audible: "Burns beats his wife," he murmured.

Fairchild sat with the *F*s, in alphabetical arrangement,

third row from the front. I sat at the back among the Ws. The only thing behind me was an upright piano. But I could hear George Fairchild. The words had a wizard effect on me, such cool impertinence. "Burns beats his wife."

Like a running fire the music flew around the room. Boy after boy bowed his head as if in concentration, covered his mouth, and chanted: "Burns beats his wife. Burns beats his wife." Dum, da-da-*dum!* (Pause.) Dum, da-da-*dum!* (Pause.)

Albert Burns froze at the chalkboard, listening, his arm held midstroke. There was sunlight from the windows on the left-hand side; it spilled his shadow long and lengthwise on the board. Suddenly he whirled around and whined, "I do not!"

"Burns beats his *wife!*" (Pause.) "Burns beats his *wife!*" (Pause.)

"Do you—" Albert Burns whined against the waves of chanting, "do you know the meaning of Christian love? Jesus loved the people. Jesus never hardened his heart, never hardened his face to the people. Jesus abhorred—"

"Burns beats his *wife!*" Boom! "Burns beats his *wife!*" Boom!

The classroom jumped to the percussive rhythm. Boys were drumming their desks to the chant. It was astonishing to me how directly they looked into Burns's eyes, unflinching, unabashed, in perfect harmony with one another. Many were grinning. George Fairchild had the gift of high, etched eyebrows, skull-close hair, a totally emotionless face. Nothing in that boy. Nothing. Neither remorse nor delight. He was not smiling. He looked indifferent, rather—and I feared him.

"*Burns beats his wife!*" Boom! "*Burns beats his wife!*" Boom!

"This is wrong," cried Albert Burns. "This is sinful! This is disrespectful! It isn't Christian! You're studying to be pastors! Why won't you listen to me? What's the matter with—"

I remember these words. I remember with dead accuracy

his efforts at command and self-esteem. The memory is
nailed in my mind by the scene that followed: Albert Burns
was annihilated.

He cried, "What's the matter with—" and choked on the
last word, *with*. His mouth gaped open, fixed that way. For
a moment his whole body seemed a statue. But then it
looked as though he were physically assaulted by grief. He
sucked air through his open mouth. His face twisted and
turned a furious red. His brow crept upward, and all at once
his eyesight flooded.

Burns walked toward the back of the classroom. I watched
him come. He sat on the piano bench behind me, laid his
left arm on the keyboard, bowed his head, and wept. The
tears soaked into the thick hair of his forearm.

Burns beats his wife!

He was annihilated, brought to nothing. And all by the
words of my classmates. Why hadn't he stormed from the
room? But he hadn't. And I had learned the lesson (however
tiresome this adolescent slander seems to me now) that contempt can cause the man to *be* contemptible. Moreover, I
extrapolated: if they could bring down a full-grown man,
what could they do to me? Or what were they doing already,
more than I knew, more than I was willing to admit? What
sort of figure did *I* cut in this place?

There was some pity in me for Albert Burns, crouched at
the keyboard, crying. But only some. I was a boy engaged
in survival, and I was thunderstruck at the pure power of
derision. Had I feared in the past that I might shrink away
to nothing? Well, here were people who could do it to me
on purpose, who murdered with malice and smiles, without
remorse, by scorn alone. Concordia. My boarding school. My
gross environment. The world.

And so it was that after the Christmas holidays that year,
precisely as my parents drove me across the Twenty-Seventh
Street viaduct, I took sick.

I glanced from the window of the car. I saw the Red Star

Yeast sign lurid in the night, expanding, contracting around its clock, and I felt a rush of loathing so strong that I began to shiver. After two weeks in Chicago, surrounded by my family and firelight and carols and the New Year's Eve and safety and security, I was returning to the dorm and to Concordia. The star confirmed it.

Just then the musty smell of hops crept in the car. The brewery odor, fermentation, the warm humus of Milwaukee trickled down my throat. I gagged. I vomited bile. I held this acid behind my teeth and swallowed it by bits, quietly, quietly. But here was a symptom the child could not deny. I was sick.

I said nothing to my father, who helped me carry luggage to my room, or to my mother when we said good-bye. But as soon as they left, I went to the infirmary for the first time that year. The nurse received me. She assigned me a bed, and I fell immediately into a fitful sleep. I slept for three days, dreaming.

2.

I grew conscious of a breathing at my left ear, the steady whistling of nostril hair and narrow sinuses. I was waking up. Someone's face was very close to mine. I moved, and the breathing stopped. In a moment it started again. Then I must have dozed some more.

All at once I was wide awake, and I opened my eyes.

There was a boy beside my bed, sitting on a chair and staring at me. For just an instant he seemed lost in thought; but then he realized that I was looking back at him, and he snapped upright. Guilt stung his eyes. He opened his mouth and produced the most curious honking giggle, his eyebrows flipping up and down as if to say, *See? See? What a silly fellow am I!*

"You're awake," he said, clasping his hands. "Good! Do you know how long you've been out? Oh, a long time, a long

time. You'd be surprised at how long you've been sleeping!"
Even so quickly did the boy's face shake off guilt. Now it
was full of tics and wiggles, animation: it was difficult to read
which mood was there, since one followed so quickly upon
the other, a frown, dismay, a knowing grin. The boy had a
larval face, squirming, bedroom-pale with stark black brows.
"I guess you're sick, hey? *Honk! Honk!* Not dodging classes,
faking it. No one could fake sleep that long—unless you're
a marathon faker. *Honk!* Like the man of a thousand faces.
Did you see that movie with Lon Chaney? You talk in your
sleep, you know that? Listen, you want some tea?"

Tea? What? Who drinks tea?

I must have frowned.

"No, that's okay. I can make it," said the boy, his face a
quilt of apologies, solicitation, pride. "I've got my own elec-
tric pot and teabags and cups. You want some tea? It's no
trouble, really. You want some? I'll make you some."

He hopped up from the chair and bustled to the bedstand
next to mine. He lifted a little pot on high, hanging with a
rat's tail cord. He winked. "Water," he explained, and bustled from the ward.

He was wearing two-piece pajamas, creased down the pant
leg. Apparently he occupied the bed to my left. There were
eight beds altogether in the long room, four facing four;
but six were tightly made with fat, unwrinkled pillows. We
were the only patients. I think it must have been late in the
afternoon; a wintry declining light came through the windows on my right. The single door was to my left.

That boy had said something that stuck in my brain, both-
ering me. What did he say? A menacing thing. It made me
feel vulnerable. It made me want to talk with him some
more, to question him—

Oh! He said I talked in my sleep! No, I didn't like that,
because what was I revealing to someone I didn't know? And
it caused a distressful sense of intimacy with this boy, to

think that he had heard my dreams, that he had crept into my sleep. I didn't want to be close to anyone at school. I didn't like that.

On the other hand, there's a powerful curiosity about one's own self, something flattering in a conversation that focuses with interest upon one's subconscious self. I wondered what I said in my sleep.

The nurse came in, stout and starched, Grandma Efficiency.

"Horstman told me you woke up," she said. She came to the side of the bed and placed her hand on my forehead, then her knuckles on my cheek. I liked that. She took a thermometer from my bedstand and shook it. "You brought a bug from home, what?" she said. "But we'll put a little broth in you and you'll be right. Under your tongue, Walter."

"Is it all right to drink tea?" I asked. I cleared my throat. My voice was thick with mucus.

"Tea, what? You want tea?"

"Well—no. I mean, I don't mind. He went to make some."

"Who? Horstman?"

"I guess so."

"Daniel Horstman! He thinks the infirmary's his dormitory, poor lad! Tea? It's as good as anything for a starter. Under your tongue."

I allowed the invasion of her thermometer and bit down. The nurse bustled from the ward. Why did it annoy me that tea was as good as anything? Why did I want this boy—Horstman?—to be wrong? I didn't like his presuming things. I wanted to say—not, "I don't want tea," since that would be too bold—but, "The nurse said I can't have tea." That would be protected by the rules, and Horstman would have run foul of the nurse, not me.

But here came Horstman, *slop, slop,* in slippers, dripping water from his teapot.

"It snowed outside while you were sleeping," he said, kneeling down to plug the cord into the wall. "You're Wangerin, right? Tillie told me."

"Tillie?"

"Tillie Pfund. The nurse. You didn't know? I knew. We're in the same class, you and me, different tracks, but you probably know me since most of the guys know me, and now I know you too. Wally Wangerin." He sat down on the edge of his bed, facing me, smiling, frowning, constantly switching expressions.

He had no right to call me Wally.

I turned away from him. I was beginning to feel sick again, a tingling in dry skin.

"You want me to read your temperature?" he said.

I shook my head. Horstman. Horstman. He was right—I had heard of him before. When? And this skinny restlessness of his seemed familiar, but I couldn't remember the context. I had very little conversation with other boys. I would have had to *over*hear his name. Daniel Horstman.

"You want me to plump your pillow?" he said behind me, and then, to my amazement, he reached right over my head with his left arm—so close that I could smell hair tonic— and began to squeeze my pillow between his hands.

This caused a storm of feelings inside me. "Don't!" I cried, shrinking from him. "Don't do that!" Spitting around the thermometer.

"What?"

"Don't. I'm all right."

"What?" said Horstman, his voice suddenly so tiny that I looked at him. His face, too, was tiny. He was pinched right down to a miserable blister. He had snatched his hands behind his back.

I must have shouted at him. In spite of myself, I felt sorry to be cruel to Horstman.

"Now, now, Horstman, let the poor lad rest," said the nurse, returning to the ward. "Here, Walter, let me see that."

She took the thermometer from my mouth. "Um-mm. One oh one. Not bad, not bad. But you'll be with us till it's normal. One full day without a fever, and then you go. Rest. Rest. I'll bring you broth and a bit of Jell-O in a while."

She left. She was snow-light and cleanliness. I would have to go to the window and look at the snow outside. I liked snow. I took comfort in the bed of winter and the purging cold. But I wouldn't get up now. I didn't want to give this Horstman some signal for talking after the nurse said, "Let him rest," meaning me.

Horstman.

Was sitting straight up on his bed, staring forward. Pouting, I think. Or else was truly wounded and suffering.

Daniel *Horstman!* Yes! I remembered him!

Several weeks into the fall term there had been a banquet in the refectory, a gathering of students, all strangers in dark suits. There was beef and potatoes and corn, labored, rhetorical speeches—all of it heavy, oppressive to me. I, too, wore a suit and a choking tie. Someone had played the piano during the meal. He played a long, dramatic piece which descended from sweetness to declarative force, then rose to a lush and nearly impossible sweetness again. I had paid attention to that music. I let it make a space for me in the refectory, and I marveled that one so young could play with such dexterity, that he could play all by himself in the corner of the room while no one, apparently, listened, while everyone was talking and eating. That musician had been Daniel Horstman.

The teapot whistled on his bedstand. The boy in bed, pianist's hands in his lap, didn't move.

"Horstman," I said.

"What." He stared straight forward.

"The tea."

"Well, I expect you don't want any."

"The nurse said it's as good as anything for a starter."

"You mean Tillie Pfund."

"Yes."

"You want a cup of my tea, Wally?" He looked at me, such naked appeal breaking his face that I turned my eyes aside, to the wall, to the singing teapot.

"That'll be fine," I said.

"Orange Pekoe?" he said so tentatively—as though Orange Pekoe might be another mistake—that I couldn't tell him I had no idea what Orange Pekoe meant.

I said, "What was the music you played at the banquet in September? What kind of music was that?"

The boy burst with a radiant light. "See? See? I told you most of the guys know me. And that's a reason!" He bounded from bed, unplugged the pot, shook teabags from their packages, and poured steaming water over them in separate cups—all the while grinning with enormous pleasure, frowning clouds of meditation, twisting his face in spasms of worry, grinning again.

He handed me a cup on its saucer. "Rachmaninoff," he said politely.

"What?"

"Rachmaninoff's Rhapsody on a Theme by Paganini. That's what I played at the banquet."

Reinking came to see me in the infirmary. I was shocked. I hadn't even imagined my roommates noticed my absence. That one of them should actually visit me was a charity so unexpected that it flustered me. I blushed and couldn't speak well.

"What," I stuttered. "What are you doing here?"

"Brought you assignments," said Reinking, sizing up the room, the ward. "Somebody had to. Professors are saying, 'Where's Wangerin?' We're saying, 'Who knows? He don't tell us where he goes.' But I figured it out you were sick. How you doing, Wangerin?"

"Not bad. Not bad." I was embarrassed by the intensity of

my gratitude. In that instant I loved Bob Reinking—or felt something approaching love, though this athlete, this tennis player with his bowlegs and rolling shoulders would snort and drop to locker-room language if he had the least idea what I felt. *Girl,* he'd say with a distancing sneer. Therefore I struggled for the impassive face, protecting myself, experiencing fear and pleasure all at once. "Tillie Pfund says my temperature is going down. Two days, maybe three days yet."

"Well, it's five days now."

"Wow."

"Freedom, Wangerin. We got freedom without your gloomy puss in the room, criticizing everything."

"Reinking, I don't—"

"Relax. Just joking. You're all right. But he's not—hoo, boy!"

Reinking was referring to Horstman, who had just left the ward.

Horstman had sat bolt upright at my roommate's boisterous entrance, and then had fixed his face toward the far wall, controlling the tics and wiggles with a mighty effort, his lips gone white. Suddenly he'd thrown back the covers, put on his slippers with grave formality, and gone *slop, slop* from the ward. Grim.

"How can you sleep," hissed Reinking, "with that fairy next to you? I'd watch it, Wangerin. I'd keep a careful eye on those greasy hands if I were you," he said, shifting weight from foot to foot.

My stomach constricted at Reinking's opinion. My face strove for slackness, the passive, noncommittal expression, cool unconcern. "Oh yeah?"

"Oh yeah," said Reinking on the balls of his feet. "Why do you think he stays up here all the time?"

"I don't know." Oh no! Guilt by association. But I really am sick, Reinking.

"I don't know either. All I know is, his roommates don't

want him flitting round *their* room in the night. I think,"
leered Reinking, "they make life difficult for him. Ha, ha!
I've seen him sit with that stone face on his bed two hours
at a time. Ha, ha! Poor Danny Horstman. We don't do you
like that, do we, Wangerin?"

By the time Bob Reinking departed, my feelings of gratitude had turned to water and fear.

Then Horstman returned to the room and sat on the side
of his bed, staring at me—the same, I thought, as he must
have stared while I was sleeping. It unnerved me. I pretended to be reading. But my ears were hot.

"You talked in your sleep last night," said Horstman, staring.

"Hum," I said, reading.

But I felt a rush of anger. To bring up that intimacy now,
just now, seemed to me simply perverse.

"You want to know what you said?"

"No."

"You said, 'Look out! Look out!'" said Horstman. "You
shouted it. You sounded scared."

"Hum."

"What do you suppose was scaring you, Wally?"

He had no right to call me Wally.

"Do you remember any dreams from last night?"

"Uh-uh."

He had no right to call me Wally, and he had no business
in my fears *or* my dreams. This was private. This was the
desperate preservation of myself at the boarding school,
Concordia. If I cried *Look out* in my sleep, then I was revealing a weakness I wanted no one, no one to know about—
least of all Horstman. I didn't want to join my weakness with
the weak. And Reinking's opinion—

"Aren't you going to talk to me?" said Horstman coldly,
staring at me.

"Well," I said. "I'm reading now, you see—"

"Wally! *Wally! Wally!*" he shrieked.

This jolted me. This was a purely anguished wail. Horstman had actually clasped his hands before his breast in a begging gesture, and his face was swarming with tics of appeal. He stunned me, so blatant was the pleading.

"Wally, talk to me!" he cried. "I'm on an all-campus blackout. I am! I know I am! And what was Reinking doing here? He told you to black me out too. Talk to me!"

Daniel Horstman was suffering—so undisguised a suffering that it frightened me. The reality might have been exaggerated, but not the feeling. This was no hypocrisy. This was uncontrol.

"I don't," I whispered, "I don't know what blackout means."

"Silence!" he cried, jumping up and beginning to pace the middle of the room. "Nobody will talk to me. But I had to do what I had to do. Wally, you're sensitive, you're good. You can see that?"

"Dan, I don't know what you did."

"You don't?" he roared almost angrily, lifting his lip with suspicion. "Then you're the only one."

"I promise you, I don't. I don't know what you're talking about."

He stared at me a while, then dropped his face into his hands. Long fingers. Trembling fingers, and white. He took a deep breath, then threw himself to pacing again and poured forth his miserable story.

On the Tuesday before Thanksgiving, he and a boy named Bucknell—a massive boy, a jock as big as his father; I remembered both the father and the son—had gone to Sherman Park, some distance from campus, and had met a girl there in the night. Bucknell had arranged the meeting. Bucknell had plans.

After some talk, during which Bucknell was running his hand up and down the girl's arm and bumping his body against hers, he invited her into the trees alone with him. "Horstman, you stay here," Bucknell said. "If anyone comes strolling by, you whistle."

"Whistle," Daniel Horstman said to me. "That's exactly what he meant, that I should whistle." He shook his head. "I don't even know how to whistle, but he didn't ask me that. I didn't know what they were going to do."

But what they were doing soon became terribly audible to Horstman. The girl was giggling among the trees. Bucknell was murmuring. Leaves began to crunch. Then came a breathless silence. And then came moans that disemboweled poor Horstman, who realized that he was standing watch for the act of sex.

That's how he characterized it: the act of sex. Horstman was truly miserable as he told me this.

Well, Bucknell came out of the trees alone.

"She's yours," he said to Horstman. "It's your turn now."

Daniel Horstman was unmanned by the thought. He said something formal and inane, like "Thank you, no thank you." And he fled. He literally took to his heels and raced the whole way back to Concordia as though the devil with a blackened tongue were after him. And then he spent Thanksgiving in a moral, emotional tumult.

"What could I do? What could I do?" Daniel Horstman pleaded with me. "What else could I do? Nothing else and still be right. Do you understand that, Wally? Please, please, understand that."

Upon returning to school from the holidays, Horstman had gone to the dean, the square-jawed, crease-faced bull of a dean, and reported the "act of sex" in Sherman Park. He named Bucknell.

Bucknell's father was a Lutheran pastor. And this is why I remember the two of them, father and son: early in December half of Wunder Hall was hanging out the windows, a silent audience of boys' heads, full of awe and watching. We were watching the sidewalk that traveled from the administration building, past the front of the refectory, to the downstairs doors of Wunder. And then we saw them coming, side by side, saw one of them stern as Jehovah, the other abashed and lacking his swagger. Bucknell and his father, coming to get Bucknell's luggage. The boy had been expelled, and I remember waves of sympathy in me for him, because he was walking to the execution. The man beside him looked capable of a great rage.

"You did that," I said.

Horstman nodded. "I didn't know what else to do. I wish I hadn't. But I did."

This boy was thin, not sturdy. This one was pale and twitching with incessant tics, not full of strut as were the jocks. This one, Horstman, was desolated, and I felt something for him too. Pity. A squeamish sort of pity. Not the awful sympathy as for the heroic fall of Bucknell. Pity like worms in my breast, and at the same time irritation that I should have to feel this way—and, at the same time, fear to be so involved. Something about Horstman seemed dangerous to me.

"Daniel," I whispered. I didn't say, *I'm sorry.*

He sat down on the edge of his bed and stared at me. "Wally," he said. "Can I make you a cup of Orange Pekoe tea? You liked the last one, didn't you?"

Poor, pitiful Daniel Horstman. Behold: I was larger than someone else on campus. Someone was according me a sort of stature.

"Yes," I said.

"Good!" cried Horstman, leaping up, grabbing the teapot. "Good! Good! Good! And I'll tell you what. When we get out of here, I'll play you Rachmaninoff's Rhapsody, and I'll give you the music if you want it. Good!"

Well. Maybe. Maybe not.

For the rest of that day, Horstman and I talked. Horstman did most of the talking. He distressed me more than he knew by describing his roommates' abuse of him, distressed me because I feared the same for myself—had, in fact, suffered some of the same and hated the reminder. He chattered passionately about his interests, his music, his home where he lived alone with his mother (for whom I felt compassion, wondering whether she knew the reputation her son had on campus—then that made me think of my own mother, and that too distressed me) because his father had died. His hands flew when he talked. He seemed miles past misery, exhilarated, breathless, bursting with goodwill toward me. I kept a wary physical distance. But I did not discourage the talk. Poor, pitiful Daniel Horstman.

He hardly slept that night.

I did. Deeply.

By morning the nurse announced that I was free of fever and would be dismissed the following day, Saturday. I ate a large breakfast.

But then I began to think of returning to my dorm room and classes, and I grew quiet. It wasn't exactly on me yet, but I felt the black mood coming. The fear of the wars, and the weariness of constant shelling. I ate very little lunch. And I made one critical mistake.

"What's the matter?" Horstman said to me, returning compassion and fellowship for all that I had given unto him.

I said, "I don't want to go back"—and instantly regretted saying anything.

Horstman pulled a long and knowing face, as though to say, *I understand,* and, *We two suffer the Philistines together.*

No! We do not suffer together. No, we are different, you and I. I am not like you.

In that same moment Nurse Tillie Pfund pumped into the ward, followed by a student.

"Well," she said. "Here's three of you together, and all from the same class. I approve, what? It helps to keep each other company."

When she left, the student undressed, gazing at the both of us—at Horstman and me—from underneath high, etched eyebrows, from a totally emotionless face. He took a bed opposite and slid between the sheets in shorts. No pajamas. He gazed at us with a sort of effrontery. George Fairchild.

"We were just saying," said Horstman, ticcing geniality all over his face, "how Wally is nervous about going back to his dorm room—"

Oh! My face blazed. From that instant onward I despised Daniel Horstman. I was appalled by his flat stupidity, his outrageous presumption, his destruction of all I had labored for—and I hated him. I would not say another word to him.

And I didn't. I turned my back to him.

Ice came down in the ward. Winter paralyzed the room for the rest of the day.

George Fairchild, his small, nasty mouth, his close-cut hair, said nothing. His nature was to be cold, superior to any whom he met. He was serpentine.

Horstman attempted conversation a little further. I heard him say, "Well, Fairchild. The news is out. You guys sure stuck it to Bertie Burns, *honk, honk*. What did you say? Bertie hits women? Something like that? *Honk, honk*. I heard he broke right down in class—"

But Fairchild never answered.

Horstman tried the topic on me. "You're in that class, aren't you, Wally? You're in the same class with Fairchild. What happened?"

Neither did I answer. Enough damage had been done. I had no idea what Fairchild was thinking this very minute, thinking of me. Neither did I care. I despised Horstman with all my heart. I didn't move. I didn't speak. I was scared. Fairchild was gazing at me.

Burns beats his wife. (Pause.) *Burns beats his wife.* (Pause.)

In a little while Horstman beached himself and stopped talking too.

So then it was the icy silence.

I noticed, when the nurse brought us our suppers, that

Horstman had assumed the frigid position, sitting upright on his bed, his hands upturned in his lap, staring straight at the wall across from him, his lips bloodless. He didn't once touch the food that Tillie had placed in front of him, nor even look at it, so far as I knew.

Fairchild slept through supper.

I pushed my food around the plate.

We went to sleep in silence. I was getting out tomorrow.

I heard the whistling breath at my left ear. I felt body warmth. Someone was staring at me in my sleep. Someone had his face bare inches from mine.

I opened my eyes. A wintry moonlight cast shadows over everything in the ward; the moonlight on snow is a luminance. I could see Horstman beside me, kneeling at the bedside, staring. His eyes were mica.

"Wally," he whispered. "You awake?"

I looked at him, then turned away.

"Wally, please," he hissed. "Don't black me out. Please. Talk to me."

I said nothing. His breath was sour. His heat was like disease.

"Wally, whatever I did, I'm sorry. What did I do? I'll play the rhapsody for you. Is it Fairchild? We don't have to talk in front of Fairchild. And we can go off campus when we're out of here."

I said nothing. Daniel Horstman seemed incapable of not being intimate. This was horrendous language to use, perilous in a boys' school—like making dates. I set my face like flint.

"Wally," Horstman hissed directly in my ear. "For Jesus' sake! Please, please, please, please, Wally, talk to me!"

He put his hand on my shoulder then, and I rose up in revulsion, the blankets sliding off of me. In deep shadow across the room I saw the face of Fairchild, sitting up in bed and watching us, his cold eyes sunk in two black holes—and a horror shot through me.

"Kiss off, Horstman!" I cried out loud. I pushed him. He stumbled backward and fell to the floor. I shouted with a shaking passion: "Just kiss off! You hear me?"

3.

It had been a heavy snowfall—what? A week ago. The tennis courts had vanished in a smooth depth of two feet; the nets had caused drifts like windbreaks on a Canadian plain. The sidewalks had been shoveled. *Strafarbeit.* I walked between two embankments higher than my knees. The world was white, a windless white; I was assailed by whiteness.

And the air, so crystal cold, was a shock to my nostrils. To all of my features. It seemed to me that my eyeballs contracted in the cold, grew smaller, rounder, more accurate— hard marbles of a flawless glass. For one thing, they ached in the daylight. For another, I was granted in this frozen air a vision of eagle clarity. I could see each individual brick on the face of Wunder dormitory, and the texture of the mortar, and the blue sky to a distance of infinitude, and the very edges of the starched cloud lingering in that sky. I am nearsighted. Clear vision is a miracle. I felt lean in my face, austere, like Anthony in the desert. But the world was white, and the only smudge on the pure, cold atmosphere was my own breathing, which rose from my mouth in clouds.

I truly believe that I walked from the infirmary to the dorm that day with nothing in my brain, no remembering, no old knowledge, nothing. I was merely a record of immediate impressions, reflecting the world around me: white, cold, blue, brick, sky, air, snow. I made elementary deductions: the campus seemed deserted. I was the only figure laboring through the winter stillness. Why was that? Because it was Saturday. The day of my return was everyone's day of liberty, home again or trips downtown or some personal employment or study or recreation. Whatever. Administrative offices were closed. School business stalled on a Saturday. And the holidays were past, of course, the air of expectation gone, replaced by nothing, by the season of ascesis. Winter.

Wunder too was cavernous and empty. Its halls seemed vaulted to me in those days. My steps echoed on the stairs. I was neither happy nor unhappy. Let me see; I carried my books and papers under my left arm, the stuff that Reinking had brought me. The notion flitted through my mind that I might check my mailbox in the administration building. Or else—I hadn't had a decent shower in a week. Whatever. My legs were trembling from three flights of stairs. I was unused to physical exertion.

My room was 314, halfway down the hall.

It was clean. Even through the window, as I unlocked the door, I saw sunshine skimming the tiled floor, beds made to the bounce of a quarter, blankets squared at the corners. Between my bunk and my desk sat all my Christmas luggage, still unopened. I'd forgotten about that. There was a metal packing case, in which laundered clothes would be neatly folded, and a box of Heath toffee bars, which my mother always included as a gift, a surprise (*don't think about that! It'll kill you! Evidence of your mother's love—here—you're not prepared yet! It'll kill you with pity!*).

I decided I wouldn't unpack the luggage till later. When there was some noise in the dorm. Some other life. Boys would be returning in the dusk before supper. They'd switch on a warmer light and shout or sing. Whatever. I took my coat off and dropped it, feeling rubbery in my knees.

My room too was deserted. I said it was clean; but Reinking, whose desk was in the opposite corner from mine, always left some junk on the floor. He had a constitutional inability to put everything away—like the child who *must* leave two swallows at the bottom of the glass, four beans, and a bite of meat on the plate. Like a dog's scent, maybe.

Like a signature: mine. Me. I am here. Or like one stubborn infraction to prove you're not completely subject to the law: I'm my own man! Boy. Reinking was a boy, fourteen years old.

I opened his closet. A whole gymnasium of junk fell out of it. Leather mitts. Plastic shoulder pads. Jerseys. Balls of various sizes and composition and bounce. A hockey stick, for heaven's sake! Ice skates. I picked up a tennis ball and bounced it against the door. It came back to me. I bounced it again, and it came back. I rooted in Reinking's junk and found his tennis racquet. When I held the racquet straight up, it just brushed the ceiling. So I swung it underhand and popped the ball toward the door. When it came back I hit it again. I was trying to find the "sweet spot" of the racquet, where, when you hit it right, you feel no torque at all, just the perfect *thock* of a well-placed ball, no waste of energy. But you can't swing timidly to find the sweet spot. You have to risk speed and a solid hit. I swung hard. I caught the ball squarely in the center of the netting, barely felt the weight of the ball, leveled it straight toward the door—

—and smashed its window.

I gaped at the thing I had done.

My Savior!—I'd shot that ball dead center in the hallway window, that's what I'd done. I'd punched a raw hole in the window. The glass had rained outside the door, a tinkling music on the stone floor, chimes inappropriate to the horror that spouted inside of me.

"Oh no!" I whined. "Oh no!"

Now there was thought. Now my brain was afire with thought. I was wide awake and wild with remembering: *No tennis in the dorm room! None!*

I do not remember dropping the racquet, but I must have.

Thought: that I had done it. Thought: that I had, yes, screwed up! Thought: that I was no better than any iniquitous, leering student on this campus, dear Jesus Christ! Thought: that I was a liar, a liar, in every way a liar, unworthy of my parents' trust in me, a craven, unrighteous, and damnable liar. My work was in ruins, all my goodness gone. And the fact of it all was before me—the shattered window.

It couldn't have been five seconds before I heard a door open and then shut down the hallway. I wasn't alone. I listened to the whip-crack of the shoe heel coming. Thought: that I was about to be caught, accused, and punished.

I broke my stance and ran forward. So little time, so little time. I thrust my right arm through the window hole, shut my eyes, pierced the flesh on a point of glass, then jerked the whole arm sideways. A clean cut. A deep and easy cut.

And then I stood there with my head down, my heart racing to death, awaiting the proctor with my arm through the window as though through a sling.

I was not wrong, and I was not surprised. It was the proctor indeed who came strolling down the hall unhurried. I saw his horsey nose approach the splintered glass, heard his shoes grind glass. He just looked at things without a word. He looked at me.

"I," I offered. "I," I explained with swallowings and sand in my voice. "Tripped."

The proctor nodded, noncommittal.

A flow of blood had sprung from my arm. Corroboration. It encouraged me. There wasn't the slightest sense of pain. In fact, I hadn't considered that there might be pain.

"I ran," I said. I pointed behind me. "I was coming from—"

Lord! There was the tennis racquet, lying in sunlight on the floor. So my story was false in my teeth. But I was a liar, a liar. I told it anyway.

"I ran," I said with hopeless flatness, "sort of in this direction, and tripped on the way. And my hand went through the window—" I just shut up.

Standing on the other side of the door, the proctor took my wrist and turned the arm to see the laceration.

"But it's cut across," he said.

I was bleeding a lattice of blood down the glass, stripes of a running blood all down the wood of the door. That ought to count for something. Punishment. Compassion. I was grateful he chose to talk about the cut and nothing else.

And I wanted dearly to agree with him, whatever he said. "Yes," I said, missing his implication. "The cut's across."

He nodded. Wordlessly he opened the door. I drew my arm away and held it in my left hand. All at once the blood began to embarrass me because it didn't magically stop. It potted the floor, making a mess. It streaked my pants, ran down the toes of my shoes. Wordlessly the proctor pulled a T-shirt from Reinking's junk and wound it round my arm. He put four fingers over the laceration and squeezed so tight I thought this was his anger at me. But wordlessly he walked me down the stairs and out the dorm, along the sidewalk in snow to the infirmary.

By the time we found Tillie Pfund, the T-shirt was soaked, bright as a red bandanna. And I was humiliated to be returning so soon—the second time that year, the same day I had left the place.

"I thought I discharged you," said Tillie Pfund. Then she saw the bleeding and she said no more. She became lean with efficiency and speed.

"Oh!" she murmured when she had unwrapped the T-shirt.

I had done that too—that cut. She said, "Oh," and I was mortified by shame.

But it is required that I record the entire truth—and this story is not true until it's done. One more emotion seized me in that day.

While Tillie Pfund was cleaning the wound, bent close (since I was too embarrassed to tell her she'd find no slivers of glass in there), George Fairchild came and leaned against the doorjamb of the examination room. He watched for a dead five minutes, his lifted eyebrows, his drooping lids, his cold, emotionless face. I spent that five minutes feeling as though I sat on a toilet under scrutiny. I blinked furiously.

But then Fairchild folded his arms across his chest and spoke.

"I guess you know you did it to him, Wangerin," he said. I didn't understand.

"You did it right and tight," he said. "Danny boy took his teapot. Know what that means?"

I didn't.

"He left," said Fairchild, as impassive as the sky.

"Without permission," Tillie Pfund said to my arm. "Lads are growing too big for their breeches these days."

"I'd say he took off," said Fairchild. "I'd say Horstman's sneaking home this minute. What do you think, Wangerin? You should know," he said. "You are the nemesis of Daniel Horstman, erstwhile student of Concordia."

All at once I felt a rush of a new blood in my face.

Whether or not George Fairchild had the gift of reading human nature, this is the emotion such high talk caused in me: pride. A swelling pride that seemed more healing than medicines. I sat the straighter under Tillie's ministrations. I closed my right hand into a fist, expanding the forearm muscle so that my wound split wide like a red mouth smiling.

For this was the first time Fairchild had ever chosen to speak to me directly. And oh!—with how exalted a language had he acknowledged me!

11

Baby Hannah

"Is Jon coming later, then?"

"He's here."

I looked around. No one was there. "Where?"

"In the car with Hannah. He'll bring her when she wakes."

"Or when the people wake her. Or when the service starts."

"Hum."

"I'm going to put a long table in front of the fireplace. Was it a late night, Cheri?"

"Late night all night long."

"You look tired."

"She cried and I nursed her every two hours."

"Are you all right?"

"Hum."

"Did you get a good breakfast, Cheri?"

"Hum."

I should control myself. This mother resisted being mothered.

In wide arcs I dragged a table from the wall to the space in front of a great stone fireplace. The legs bratcheted on the concrete floor, filling the whole picnic shelter with an industrial racket, and Cheri winced. This table would serve as an altar. Cheri spread a bedsheet over it while I moved wooden backless benches around. I arranged them one behind the other in two sections, so they looked like the ribs of a skeleton. I tried not to scrape them on the concrete. Cheri seemed so wan. She put a jug of Mogen David wine on the sheeted table, a chalice, a paten, a tube of wafers.

She paused a moment at the tableau, her head tipped to one side, pondering. Gentle Cheri.

I went to the extreme back of the shelter, climbed a chair, and inserted a three-pronged plug into its electrical outlet. *Tappa-tappa-tappa-tappa.* The picnic shelter was enclosed with windows on all four sides; and though the roof was high enough, and though the shelter itself stood in open country some distance from the woods, yet the bodies of the members of Grace would humidify this place uncomfortably. It wasn't well built for breezes. Wherefore the huge, belt-driven fan installed in the back, which turned not fast, but batteringly: *tappa-tappa-tappa-tappa.*

Besides, I wanted the sweet scent of the morning air to greet the people when they came. Dew and green shoots. The fireplace had left a taste of lingering winter, char and cold ash.

"Do you mind if I block the door open?"

"No."

"It won't chill you?"

"No."

"Cheri, are you all right?"

We were preparing the place for the annual picnic of Grace Lutheran Church. And since our picnics, always scheduled on a Sunday, began with worship, we were preparing for worship. Cheri and I were dressed alike, both wearing black shirts with clerical collars; or else you might say we both wore black blouses with clerical collars. Pastor Cheri Johnson. Pastor Walt Wangerin. The ministers of Grace. We shuffled furniture. We gathered old Coke cups from windowsills and paper trash from corners. We pushed brooms and wiped tables and broke ice into a cooler and measured grounds into a coffeepot and chose a board for potluck dishes and generally attended to matters most sacred, as ministers of minor parishes are called to do.

And then the people began to come.

"Mornin', mornin'!"

"Hoo, what a pretty day!"

"Where do y'all want this?"

"Herman, did you bring the softball bats?"

"I told him, you turn at the F.O.P. sign on the highway, but the old boy never listens. He'll be here by the time we eat."

"Kyle, sit! Sit! Sweat this afternoon!"

"—*was blind but now I seeeee.* What? No piano in this place?"

"Pastor Cheri! Where's Hannah?"

Cheri was bowed at a small stove, fingering water in a pot and finding it warm. Now she poured the water into a glass salad bowl. And now she carried the bowl to a pedestal in front of our makeshift altar. Her face was long and as solemn as an icon.

But I wondered whether her heart wasn't beating harder than normal as she bore the water altarward. I think so. Her face is long by nature, a slender nose, an even brow, a contemplative, slow-blinking eyelid, a nunnish droop to the corner of her mouth: she has a face composed against such excitements as the harder beating of the heart. And she has a long and slender body, calm, unrevealing of heartbeats. Nevertheless, I'll bet she felt a shiver as she set the water on its pedestal—because this water was meant for a baptism.

In this particular worship service, on this particular Sunday morning, Pastor Cheri Johnson was going to baptize her baby, her firstborn child, her Hannah.

'Twas grace that taught my heart to fear—

The skeletal ribs of the benches were ribs no longer, but wonderfully, colorfully, fatly fleshed. We turned Shaker austerity into jambalaya—we black, demonstrative, broad, declamatory people! We sat and sang without piano, without our hymnals, by memory and by faith alone. Grace had gathered. Honey, shut your eyes and open your mouth. Worship had begun.

—and grace my fears relieved—

Herman Thomas Sr. sang leaning forward with both elbows on his knees, his bulk and all his round contentment hanging down between his thighs. This is a peaceable man.

Miz Lillian Lander sang from a position perfectly upright. Her face looked older than when first I met her, yet she needed no back to her bench. Her back was staunch enough. It had borne children into the world, and grandchildren, and great-grandchildren. It had borne me. It had borne the death of Douglas, and bore the memorial of her husband still. Miz Lil had a back like the rod of Moses. And she sang like Miriam.

How precious did that grace appear—

Dee Dee Lawrence, Bridgette Hildreth, Scott Tate, Rena and Michelle Gilbert, the youth of the congregation sprouted at the rear of the shelter like an unmown patch of grass.

Joseph Chapman sang with his chin tucked into his throat, on a deep bass note. Selma smiled rather more than she sang. Jolanda Jones didn't know all the verses of the hymn, but did not mind. Smoke barked like Bowzer in her lap. Tim and Mary and Herman Moore; Margaret Wiley; Linda Hudson, the mother of Kyle; Ken and Debbie Stewart, whose countenances were ethereal with spirit; Aida and James Robnett, Cherokee and Larry Johnson, Elfrieda Churchill, Gloria Ferguson, Harvey Chandler, Rita Cooksey, Sylvia Davis, all the Malones, all the Outlaws, all of the people, a goodly company, a chosen generation, a holy nation: Grace! We sang like the sigh of the dusty stars of heaven.

And Jon, the husband of Cheri—he sang softly in the ear of baby Hannah, whose head was like a wheel of cheese, who had a birthmark in the middle of her forehead, who was this morning to be baptized in the midst of the congregation.

—the hour I first believed.

When the hymn was done and the people focused forward, Pastor Cheri moved to the altar, and we proceeded through the familiar ritual, the worship that named and shaped us.

We prayed.

She said, "Let the people say—"

And the people said, "—Amen."

We read three lessons from the Holy Scripture, from Genesis, from the Epistle to the Romans, and a portion from the Gospel according to St. Matthew.

Quietly, Cheri said, "The Gospel of the Lord."

The people turned a country shelter into holiness. They answered, "Praise to you, O Christ."

We sang again.

I rose and preached. The people listened, laughed and frowned and blinked and listened.

We gathered an offering. ("Kyle, what did I tell you before?")

We sang. We know how to sing.

And then (was Cheri's heartbeat faster than usual?) Pastor Cheri walked to the pedestal, its bowl and its waiting water. Wraithlike, her face. Pale, it seemed to me. Solemn below the cheekbones.

"In Holy Baptism," said Pastor Cheri Johnson, mother of the infant, "our gracious heavenly Father liberates us from sin and death by joining us to the death and resurrection of our Lord Jesus Christ—"

So the Rite of Baptism had begun.

Jon was gazing steadfastly forward. Baby Hannah raised her wobbly head and rolled her eyes to the left and the right. Maybe she was trying to find the source of her mother's voice. A host of people in her vicinity noticed the motion and turned smitten smiles upon the child.

"We are born children of a fallen humanity," said Cheri. "In the waters of baptism we are reborn children of God, inheritors of eternal life—"

She spoke softly, formally. One could hear the click of her saliva. Perhaps her tongue was dry and tacky on the roof of her mouth.

At the appropriate moment, Jon stood. Hannah was presented—blinking over the people—as the one to receive this imminent baptism.

Cheri acknowledged the presentation by a single nod. The two of them might have been strangers.

Cheri prayed a long prayer regarding waters. "And let the people say—"

The people said, "—Amen."

And then the child came forward. And the father. And the sponsors of the child. All of the sponsors. A munificence of sponsors. Thirteen! They decimated the congregation, leaving gaps on the benches. Jon and Cheri, generally restrained in their behavior, had been prodigal in planning Hannah's baptism, bestowing on their daughter more god-parents than Jesus had disciples: young and old, male and female, black and white. Sponsors surrounded the pedestal in front of the altar. Sponsors hid from view the bowl, the baby, and the mother-pastor, Cheri.

So I heard, thereafter, what I couldn't see.

I heard Cheri's voice arise from the tight wall of bodies: "Do you believe in God the Father?" The congregation responded with the creed; the whole body of people confessed belief with tiny Hannah, whom they couldn't see. "Do you believe in Jesus Christ?" said Cheri. "Do you believe in God the Holy Spirit?" Yes, yes, they did. We did.

There was a pause. I imagined someone shifting the weight of the baby, gingerly holding her head above the water. I imagined that Cheri dipped her own slender hand into the water. And I must have been right, because she began the formula for the baptism itself.

Cheri said, "Hannah, I—"

But she paused there. She stopped right there. All she had said was "Hannah, I—" and she stopped.

We waited for the next words. We all knew the next words, so it felt like leaning forward midstride: *baptize you in the name of*—

But she'd only said, "Hannah, I—"

A silence can last a while unquestioned, but only a while. In the middle of a ritual, that is a very short while. But this silence continued, and I became aware of the fan in the back of the shelter, chattering foolishly, *tappa-tappa-tappa-tappa.*

What was the matter? I stared at the close knot of bodies around the stalled sacrament. None of them were moving. Cheri? I glanced toward the congregation. Herman Thomas, his experience slung low between his legs, smiled back at me and shrugged. He didn't know, *tappa-tappa-tappa;* but he was content to wait. Miz Lil gazed straight forward, too wise to worry what she couldn't see, blessed with an endless patience. But the youth in the back of the room were like me, awake to the silence and frowning, halfway standing to see, and seeing nothing but sponsors. *Tappa-tappa.*

I began to feel excessive urges of leadership, that I should do something, walk over and cut through the crowd and learn the trouble and correct it. Do something. I grew very uncomfortable. All she had said was, *Hannah, I—*

Cheri! What is the matter?—

Just then she spoke. I heard her voice rise up. The words were exactly the same, but her tone was different, stricken.

"Hannah," Cheri said. She had to fight to pronounce the word. It came through a constricted throat, and when it did come it was tiny as a wren, a piteous peeping.

"Hannah," she squeaked, "I baptize you in the name of the Father—"

Oh, Cheri! I understood.

She was crying.

Pastor Cheri had stopped to cry. Mother Cheri could not talk for a while because she was weeping over the baptism of her baby.

All at once I saw her—as if there were no sponsors between us at all. I saw her, crimson-cheeked and moist, her hand below her baby, her hand still sunken in the water, but her face split open with its love above the child.

Of *course* Cheri would be crying. She loved this infant whom she washed. It was hers, hers, the bursting and the blood of her own body—Cheri's. Of course she would weep at Hannah's second birth. Cheri knew birthing. She had birthed the baby the first time, and she was not ignorant of the meaning now.

Again—I saw her as if there was nothing between us, neither sponsors nor space nor time. I saw in detail that first birthing of the baby Hannah, for Cheri had entrusted me with the experience.

I saw the bedroom.

Cheri had delivered Hannah at home. She and Jon had been guided by the ministrations of a midwife. But the labor was long, and she told me that she suffered uncertainty at how the baby ought to come. She didn't know what position she should take to accomplish this holy thing.

For a long while she leaned on Jon, and they walked up and down the bedroom. The contractions made a monument of her belly, hard and hard and heavy. She groaned.

Then she kneeled at the side of the bed, like a girl-child in prayer; but the position didn't feel right.

She climbed on the bed. She lay on her back, panting and gasping her breath. The baby was coming, oh! She brought her knees up. Where do the pillows go? No, this wasn't right either. Too low. Not all of herself was in the thing. Restless, rearing Cheri! Laboring mother, trying hard in all things to be right and right for the sake of the baby—and the baby was coming.

Suddenly (so she told me and I saw it) she rose up on her knees on the bed, her knees apart to make a space for the life inside, sheets below to receive it: and she pushed down, she bowed down with all her might, and this is the way the baby was delivered. This was right. Milkweed splits its pod

to send its seed adrift. Cheri burst her womb. Hannah
slipped headfirst into the world. Hannah was born through
the tearing pain of her mother, in a rain of Cheri's blood,
but the mother never considered the pain impossible nor
the blood wrong. Blood, then: blood had bathed this baby
first!

And now the water of baptizing.

Which was a sort of sacred blood, washing Hannah whiter
than snow.

Hannah, I—

Of course this mother would weep at the baptism of her
child, her heart. She was weeping in gladness for her beloved, whom she loved not merely in sentiment, but in most
holy doing, with her bones and her blood and her muscle,
her womb and her suffering. She was weeping in knowledge—for this was a birth that no one could snatch away
from Hannah, a life forever; and this time no one suffered
pain but the Savior, no one bled but the Christ; but Cheri
knew what sort of pain that was.

Of course she would cry. Me too. Herman Thomas too,
and Jolanda Jones, and Dee Dee Lawrence. And Miz Lil. We
turned shining eyes on one another and grinned and began
to cry with mother Cheri, Pastor Cheri: *Hannah, I baptize you*
in the name of the—

But again, again—I saw Cheri as if there was nothing between us, neither time nor space nor flesh nor worlds, and
I recognized in that same moment a most celestial thing:

That *I* was the baby Hannah.

That Cheri was the figure of my God, and God was weeping.

And this is what my heart sang: Holy God, how you have
mothered me!

For the crying voice of Reverend Cheri Johnson was precious, was the voice of the Holy One, *bath qôl,* daughter of
the voice—of God! Divine the words that she uttered at this
second birthing: she was the authority of the love of God,

effectual and effectually there. Oh, this was no metaphor nor some image of my mind. This was sacred fact, present and immediate—and I saw how the weeping God had birthed me.

I saw the restless God, pacing and pacing the empyrean, suffering the contractions of my bulking incompletion, my unborn presence, suffering in the deeps and the very elements of uncreated being. I saw God searching for and finally finding the holiest, most merciful posture for bringing me to birth—

I saw the mighty God kneel down.

God knelt in utter humility for a tender parturition, tender to me, hurtful to the tender parts of God. God sank into this world, humble to all of the laws, bowed down to all of its pain. The Word became a flesh that could bleed a human blood.

And having knelt, God groaned and bore me my second time. In pain. I was born in a rain of godly blood: blood that I had caused, for I burst my God, the brow and the palms and the heart of God, in order to be born; but blood my God did not begrudge me, for this was the very life of God upon me. Wash me! Wash me clean.

And even now the maternal God remembers my delivery. I am not lost in the multitude. What mother does not remember the single deliverance of every single child she bore? What mother doesn't whisper the baby's name, remembering? So God loves me and calls me by my name.

At my own baptism, did my mother weep? Did the dear God weep when my human father, then my pastor, baptized me in Vanport, Oregon? And were the waters that washed me, head and soul, perhaps the tears of God? Is that the virtue of those waters?

So much that has fallen between that time and this—the sickness of my youth, the rude cure of my congregation, the hyssop of Grace—so much has been a cause for weeping.

Do you weep for me even now, my God, my God?

Tappa-tappa-tappa-tappa. The fan turns neither faster nor slower but louder, filling another pause in the picnic shelter. Cheri is at the long table, our makeshift altar, where I can see her now. Wan. The woman is, yes, plain and pale as a medieval saint, her nose and her whole face elongated, her body spare and unadorned. But that baby of hers is fat. Hannah is full of a sweet juice, as swollen as some imperial strawberry: rub her, and you rub the red a little redder. Pinch her, she will burst, ho-ho!

And the morning scent has filled this place. Green is the color of the smells. We know nothing of asceses. Grace surrounds wan Cheri with abundance. Fat baby, a fatter congregation, a morning of fatness—I am smiling.

With the tips of her fingers Cheri is touching the birthmark on Hannah's forehead, drawing two lines there while all the congregation stands and waits and watches: *tappa-tappa-tappa.*

Pastor Cheri breaks the silence. She says, "Hannah, child of God, you have been sealed by the Holy Spirit and marked with the cross of Christ forever."

The people nod. Yes, Grace approves. Yes: Grace agrees.

Reprise

"He never learned to drive a car, you know," Miz Lillian tells me, rocking and rocking into darkness. Neither of us minds the darkness. We welcome it, rather. And she isn't looking at me anyway. She doesn't need the light to see.

"He walked," she says. One arm is tight to the arm of her rocking chair. The other is too; but sometimes it steals to her stomach. These memories seem the lading of her womb. She is old. Miz Lil has grown so old.

"He always wanted to walk. Well, and he loved to talk, is the reason. He would talk with anyone he met, dollar-proud or penniless. I hated to send him for something I needed right now, because it didn't matter how much I hurried or harried him, Douglas would always take time to stop and talk to people. Oh, Pastor," she says in a faint, most feminine sigh. "Oh, Pastor."

I sit in the dying light of her living room, recalling her husband. My sight has settled on the dim lines of her face, the rising lids beneath her eyes which seem to float her vision upward. But her conversation is a powerful agent for remembering, and I see Douglas. I see the man in the post office exactly as I saw him waiting in line when I rushed through the door—Douglas, nodding at me as if my arrival were the very reason he'd traveled so many miles from home. I remember how he sang me to a standstill then, the temples of his silver glasses flashing, all the time in the world for his judgeless observations: *Just one o' them things.*

Even today I will sometimes think I see him standing on the sidewalk, talking; and I'll want to beep as I drive by. I don't, of course. That's sad.

Douglas Lander is dead. Miz Lil is in the rocking chair and riding into darkness, remembering him. And I—of all the children of God, I am most favored. For I came to her house prepared to minister to the woman with prayer and Holy Communion; but then she interrupted mine with a ministry of her own. Gently, almost imperceptibly in the creeping evening, she has laid aside reserve and invited me into her privacies further than ever before, further than my deserving.

The wafer between us and the tiny vial of wine are sinking into darkness. All the furniture, the forests of her photographs, the form of the woman herself are growing obscure. One line of moonlight rims her cheekbone, but she is black in blackness: Africa touched by a twilight. Africa descending.

Her voice is real. And the cricking of her chair—these things are real before me, undiminished.

"But he always came home," she says. "Late, untroubled, he always walked into the house again. He hung his hat with me. I never disputed his habits, no. Seems we never had cause to argue. Seems we just got along.

" 'Lil,' he said one evening, 'where is that pie you baked for supper?' I said, 'It's in the kitchen, Doug.' He said, 'I think I'll have some more of that pie'—"

Miz Lil pauses a moment. The rocking ceases. "What *was* that pie?" she whispers. "Mm! Why can't I remember what kind of pie that was?"

I think that it would be nice if I could help her, but I can't. I say nothing. Her effort, her blackness swell into the room. Warm.

"I was resting on the sofa, you know," she says, "where

you're sitting. Douglas was watching the television from his chair. Well, and the sound of the television always makes me sleepy. I heard him go into the kitchen and open a drawer, for a fork, I suppose—but then I must have dozed a little.

"I woke up suddenly. It wasn't any noise that woke me up. I didn't hear anything at all. That's what woke me. The quiet. I don't know how to explain it. There was such a peculiar quiet in the house, there was such a stillness on my body like I never felt before—but I felt it now.

"Douglas was lying on the floor, perfectly still. I saw the piece of pie on the arm of his chair, partly eaten, and the fork was there. He must've gotten up and was coming to tell me something; but the house was quiet now, so quiet. I can't explain that feeling to you. Between the chair and the sofa Douglas just lay down and died. I was dozing while he did that."

The living room is full of the darkness now. Miz Lil is rocking again: *crick, crick, crick.* Her shoulder keeps catching a patch of moonlight, then dropping it. *Crick, crick.* I can hear another, softer sound as well, an almost inaudible whispering of fabric—ah. She is rubbing her stomach.

"He always came back, you know," she says. "When he worked for the L & N Railroad in the dining car—it took him all the way to St. Louis, but he came back. When he worked at the Vulcan Plow Works during the Depression, he came back. I used to pack a picnic basket and carry the children on over to Sunset Park, and even if we started to eat without him, well, he would come from work. We would enjoy the scenery and then walk home and get there by bedtime. He always came back, Douglas did, always untroubled.

"But he hasn't come back this time.

"And he's left an ache like stone in my stomach.

"Pastor, the aching is always, always there."

Miz Lil falls silent.

And I draw in that same instant a breath of such startled recognition that I shudder and the breath goes out in a groan. She uses elemental images, Miz Lillian does. My hand steals to my own stomach. I recognize her stone.

Miz Lillian says, "I've gotten used to the ache by now. It's all right. It's all right. I call it a friend to me. This aching reminds me all the time of Douglas. Mm. There is a gravestone in Oak Hill Cemetery, on his grave, you know. But it's a sort of a stone in me too. The children and everyone else can mourn by that stone at Oak Hill. This one is mine. The widow's stone."

Crick, crick, crick. She rocks. She rides a gentle memory deeper into darkness.

"The doctor keeps telling me that he wants to operate on my heart," she says. "They always said that I had a poor heart, even before Douglas died. Well, and I do get tired these days, and I have to lie down more often than not. But I keep telling the doctor I don't want no cutting, I don't need no cutting. I can leave this way as well as another. Douglas and me, we got no debts."

The rocking stops. Moonlight shows me her shoulder.

"Pastor?"

"What?"

"Is something wrong?"

I lift my hands, but the darkness hides them. "No, nothing," I say.

There is a little pause before the rocking begins again, and a longer pause for rocking.

"Douglas loved to fish," she says. *Crick, crick.* "He and his friends, you know. He sometimes get a nice catch of cat fiddlers and bring them home, or blue gill, or else buffalo, we call them. Sometimes he had fisherman's luck. Cyrus Garner, George Warren, Charles Hildreth, Harlan Lee—these were some of his fishing buddies, most of them dead now. Pastor?" She has stopped rocking. I think she is leaning forward. "Pastor? Does my remembering worry you?"

"What? No, it doesn't worry me."

She waits a moment in perfect silence. Yes, she is leaning

forward: the moonlight makes a doily on the backrest of her rocker, and her dark head makes the moonlight crescent. She's peering at me.

"Pastor?"

"Yes?"

"You're crying."

"Ah, Miz Lil!"

I am. I'm crying, though I hardly realized it. These are easy, easy, relieving tears, altogether right in the presence of this woman, no noise whatsoever. I haven't sobbed. I've only allowed my tears their freedom. Then how can Miz Lil—?

"You," she whispers carefully, "loved Douglas too."

"I did. I do. I do."

"You've come to share the sorrow with me."

"I would take it from you, if I could."

"I cry sometimes even now," she whispers, still leaning forward, her head a black eclipse of the moonlight. "Alone," she whispers. "In my bed at two of a morning. Always alone."

I hear the soft rustle of fabric. Suddenly her hand is on my knee.

"Pastor, why are you crying?"

And as suddenly the truth slips from me: "Because you're talking with me."

"Oh, Pastor."

For just a moment the darkness in Lillian Landers's living room is an amnesty, and it doesn't matter that I speak with appeal, like a child and not like a pastor. "Is God," I plead, "Miz Lil—is God smiling? Sometimes he's frowning, and sometimes he's smiling. Is he smiling on me now?"

Long, long the silence extends between us while the woman must be peering at me. Fox eyes. The moonlight has slid left to the edge of her chair. Then her hand begins to pat my knee—but the patting comes strangely, as though in spasms. And then Miz Lil produces a high, tiny squeek in her throat. And then it is no squeek at all, but an unmistakable giggle. The old woman is giggling. She clutches my knee.

"Pastor! I'm sorry, Pastor," she giggles right merrrily. "You make such a pitiful picture. You mean Marie. You mean skinny Marie, don't you? You've been meditating on Marie all these years? Ever since you shut her little water off? Hee hee! I'm sorry. Hee hee! That's a long time to be sitting on the pity-pot. Hee hee hee!"

Miz Lil is trying very hard to control the sudden hilarity in her throat, or else to make it respectful. She fails both ways. She wants to toss her head with the laughter. Instead she grabs both of my hands in her own and squeezes them.

"But Marie is renting in Sweetser now," she cries. "And God quit frowning long before you quit messing up. And me, I just forgot it. Pastor!" Miz Lil is shaking, full of apology, full of delight at once. It's a devestating combination, and I start chuckling too, a rougher sort of chuckle. "Oh, my Pastor!" she squeeks. "What a terrible waste of devotion! I expect you were the only one remembering. Hum! Hee! Hee hee hee hee—"

Miz Lillian purely enjoys the joke a while. She lifts our hands up as though to make a bridge for someone to pass beneath them, as though she is showing something off. She raises our hands in a high jubilation, then drops them and slumps backward in the rocking chair.

"Hooooooo," she sighs. "Hoo, that feels so good."

And then the silence returns. Silence comes down upon us like (I say) a double portion of the Spirit—and with the silence, the mantle on the shoulders of the ancient prophetess.

Crick, crick, crick. Miz Lil is rocking again. The moon has fallen to a pool on the floor. No: the moon has arisen.

"Douglas," she says, "he knew a Jewish man that owned a coal company. He'd fill our basement with coal. If Doug had the money to pay him, it was all right. If not, he accepted

whatever money on Doug's terms. I'm talking about the Depression, you know. It was good people everywhere in those
days." *Crick, crick, crick.* "Well, and the people in charge of
the West Haven Gun Club—they hired Douglas to serve par-
ties. They would bring him home and also bring all kinds
of good food too.

"He always came back, Pastor. I think about that. Maybe
late, but never troubled," she murmurs, rocking and riding
her memory home. "He hung his hat with me."

Crick, crick.